A Stranger on My Land

Sandra Merville Hart

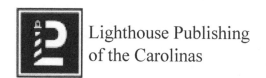

Lighthouse Publishing
of the Carolinas

A STRANGER ON MY LAND BY SANDRA MERVILLE HART
Published by Lighthouse Publishing of the Carolinas
2333 Barton Oaks Dr., Raleigh, NC, 27614

ISBN: 978-1941103272
Copyright © 2014 by Sandra Merville Hart
Cover design by writelydesigned.com
Interior design by Sherry Heinitz: www.sherryheinitz.com

Available in print from your local bookstore, online, or from the publisher at:
www.lighthousepublishingofthecarolinas.com

Brought to you by the creative team at LighthousePublishingoftheCarolinas.com: Julie Gwinn, Barb King, Rowena Kuo, Michele Creech, and Eddie Jones.

Library of Congress Cataloging-in-Publication Data
Hart, Sandra.

A Stranger on My Land / Sandra Merville Hart 1st ed.

Printed in the United States of America

Dedication

To my husband, Chris, who willingly joins me on
adventures to discover the history that brings the story.
Thank you for believing in me.

· PROLOGUE ·

rivate Adam Hendricks gripped his rifle as he stared up at Lookout Mountain. As a soldier in the Ninety-ninth Ohio Infantry, he had learned to follow orders, but the task assigned to his brigade was a daunting one. They had received orders to advance up the steep slope, over rocky ground, and toward the fortified rifle pits of the enemy. Heavy fog hid the landscape, but Adam knew what lay beyond the veil of gray. The sporadic discharge of musket fire from the pickets as they pushed up the mountain reminded him of the dangers lurking in the shadows.

Adam stared at Brigadier General Whitaker, noting an unsteadiness to his steps. Was his new brigade leader's speech a little slurred? Adam's spirits dropped even further. Whitaker wouldn't have been drinking before an attack on the enemy, would he? On the other hand, his commander would not be the first soldier to seek courage from a bottle.

Adam exchanged a concerned look with Hugh Bellamy, a close comrade, then returned his attention on their leader.

Whitaker seemed jovial enough as he addressed his men,

confident they would win the upcoming battle. He invited his men to share a drink at his quarters afterward.

Adam appreciated Whitaker's confidence in them but had his doubts about what lay ahead. He bowed his head in a quick plea for protection, then fell in line as his regiment followed Brigadier General Geary's division up the mountain.

His unit maneuvered around and over jagged rocks, trampled down bushes, and plunged deeper into dense woods. Ahead, the "pop-pop" of gunfire became more frequent. Cannons boomed from atop the summit, their shells exploding near by. Onward they marched. Their advance became a serpentine line of blue as infantry climbed their way up the steep incline. A few paces further and his regiment was ordered to turn north toward the Tennessee River. They crossed a creek and came upon a group of over forty Confederate pickets, all captured by Geary's division's sudden thrust up the mountain.

A break in the mist revealed open ground on the north slope and strong fortifications in front. The rest of the division came up quickly, forming a line from the base of the upper picket line to the mouth of the Chattanooga Creek. Flashes of gunfire marked the forward elements of the Confederate line. Geary's division slogged forward, driving the enemy from the breastworks. Union troops advanced up the slope, staggered under deadly musket fire, regrouped and pushed on. Grape and canister fire from Confederate artillery opened large holes in their lines. Men fell, others rushed forward to take their place.

By two o'clock the clouds, which had obscured the top of Lookout most of the day, became so thick General Hooker ordered Geary's division to halt. The men in Adam's regiment took cover in a ravine to wait for better light. Only once did the fog lift enough for him to see a whitewashed frame house with its long porch. Adam remembered his commanding officer comment earlier about the Cravens' house and how it might serve as a rally point for their final assault.

Adam took cover behind a log. On his commander's orders he took aim and fired into the mist. Instantly, Confederates returned fire. The fog and its gentle rain provided a false sense of protection from the deadly hail of lead. Though neither army could see the other, Brigadier General Whitaker's men continued firing into the fog. Adam felt something tug at his sleeve. At first he thought it was Hugh trying to get his attention but when he looked back he saw he remained alone. Then came the searing pain. He checked his arm. He'd been struck just above the elbow. Already the blue fabric of his uniform was reddish brown with blood. He dropped lower behind the log to inspect the wound. It hurt but didn't bleed too badly. He tried to reload his rifle and found the arm worked fine.

"You hit, Adam?" Hugh called to him amidst the dense thicket of trees.

"My arm. But it's not too bad. Just grazed me." He managed to wiggle his fingers to demonstrate.

Hugh grinned at him with approval. "Keep your head down."

"You, too."

Steady musket fire from the enemy kept him pinned behind the log. Hours passed with neither side giving ground. The mist turned into a steady shower. The expanding stain of blood mixed with rain made his injury appear worse than it felt. Adam avoided looking at it.

Dusk and fog swallowed the last rays of sunlight. Darkness seemed to amplify the sharp report of musket fire from the enemy. Neither side advanced, nor did they give ground. He could tell from the screams of his comrades that the Confederate fire was having an affect. He watched for a flash from the opposing line, aimed, and fired. He had no way of telling if he hit anything. Gradually dusk deepened into night. Raindrops froze on contact. Adam's clothes were soon coated with ice. He shivered. His wounded arm ached. He wished now he'd taken more time to check on the injury. Maybe the musket ball did more damage than he'd supposed.

The steady rain and his own shivering drowned out all but the screams of men moaning around him.

Ahead in the forest a twig snapped. He rose up to fire. Before he could swing his musket at the phantom figure, a musket ball smashed into his upper arm, spinning him around. His rifle fell from his hands. Thoroughly dazed, he groped in the darkness for his weapon. His comrades fired off a few rounds at the approaching line, but it only drew more fire. Fumbling blindly about, Adam found his rifle, but his right arm dangled by his side. A searing pain radiated from his shoulder and down to his arm and chest.

Following Hugh's advice, Adam kept his head down and crawled away from the gunfire. Getting captured would serve no purpose. He'd seek medical help then return to his unit. His kepi fell off his head when he crashed into a bush but he didn't stop to search for it. At last he reached a gully that offered some protection from the shots flying overhead. He stood, felt faint, and fell against a tree for support. Surely the rear of their line had to be close. Only a few more paces, maybe half a mile at most.

But first he needed to rest. He dropped to the ground and leaned against the rough bark of a tree.

He lost track of time.

Musket fire died away.

Twice he thought he heard men tromping through the woods but he was too weak to call out. Exhausted, he closed his eyes.

The pain in his shoulder awoke him. The rain had stopped. The sky had cleared.

As he looked at the full moon, shadows crossed it until an eclipse totally hid it. Could this be an omen, he wondered? The awe-inspiring sight might have moved him more if he hadn't been so cold and thirsty. He remembered the poncho tied to the knapsack on his back. Reaching around with his left hand, he slipped it off his shoulder, groaning as the knapsack jarred his right arm.

It took a couple of minutes for him to undo the ties that bound the poncho, but at last he arranged the waterproof cloth over his body. The blanket tied to the knapsack was drenched and of no use to him. A thirst stronger than any he had ever known assailed him. Though he knew he should conserve the little bit of water in his canteen, he drank it all and still longed for more.

Severe pain robbed him of the ability to sleep. Shifting to a prone position under the relative protection of the leafless tree, he waited. No one would find him tonight, but his friends would come in the morning.

Or so he hoped.

· CHAPTER ONE ·

Lookout Mountain, Outside of Chattanooga, Tennessee,
Wednesday, November 25, 1863

As the sound of a hundred firing muskets echoed across the valley, Carrie Bishop stepped out of the darkness of the cave that had sheltered her family for over two months. Peering left and right before replacing the branches that obscured the mouth of the small cave, she felt grateful for the wispy fog. It should help to mask her movements from any watchful eyes in the valley. Leaving the safety of the shrubs and one tall oak tree that further hid the entrance, she exhaled with relief to find no sign of the soldiers on Lookout Mountain. A noisy battle had taken place here yesterday.

Leaves rustled behind her. "Can I come out there with you, Carrie?"

Turning swiftly at her little brother's loud whisper, she motioned him back inside. "No, Jay. I told you to wait for me."

"Aw, come on, Carrie. I don't want to stay with Aunt Lavinia." Her nine-year-old brother raised his eyebrows imploringly.

Carrie sighed. They'd both been stuck inside too much lately, and their bedridden aunt's bitter complaining didn't make returning to the cave such a pleasant prospect. "Let me look around first.

I'll be right back."

Keeping her slim frame below the top of the bushes to hide from any curious eyes in the valley or across it on Missionary Ridge, she crept about twenty feet away from the cave, her eyes darting in every direction without finding any sign of the blue-clad soldiers that had so terrified her during their approach yesterday.

The Confederate Army had been on the mountain for a couple of months, causing no end of trouble for her. When the family's only horse had disappeared, Carrie had vowed the soldiers wouldn't get the cows and chickens too. They moved the livestock inside the cave with them. They'd managed to keep all the animals safe so far.

Yesterday afternoon, it seemed that most of Lookout Mountain had been crawling with soldiers, Confederates and Union alike. Jay had wanted to sneak outside the relative safety of their temporary home to see the battle, but Carrie couldn't allow it. She lived in constant fear that the hidden opening to their cave would be discovered by soldiers from either side. After the Southern Army stole her horse, it created a hardship for her family. She hadn't felt good about them since that day. As for the Northern Army, they were the reason her papa had to leave home and fight for General Lee's Confederate Army in far-off Virginia. She had a stomach full of both armies, with little tolerance left for either.

Aunt Lavinia's bitterness exceeded her own. Only she blamed Abe Lincoln's Union Army as the source of all her woes, including her poor health.

The big battle fought on the mountain yesterday had frightened her more than anything else that happened since the beginning of the war. Much of it seemed to come from the direction of the Cravens' house. Part of the fighting between the Confederate Army and the Yankee soldiers took place not far from her family's cabin, empty now of all food and as many possessions as they could carry. She'd heard stories of hungry soldiers taking food from families. Not knowing how long the war would last, she had none to spare. If any soldier found their hiding place, there would be no way to conceal their food. And her family would starve without it.

She and Jay had spent most of yesterday near the mouth of the cave, listening to cannon blasts and musket fire. They could peer through the carefully placed branches that obscured the entrance to the cave, but dense fog had covered the mountain. Since Carrie's home was about a third of the way up the mountain, most of yesterday's fighting took place above them. At times, the shouts had been far too close for comfort, though the men had been too far away to distinguish any words. That's when Carrie prayed the hardest. She asked God to hide them and keep them safe. So far He'd done that. No one had found them.

Higher up the mountain, the battle had continued until late into the night when the musket fire finally decreased. Until the shooting died down, Aunt Lavinia had fretted aloud they'd all be killed. After Aunt Lavinia quieted down in her bed across the room, Carrie had fallen into a troubled sleep. Worry awakened her several times. The battle hadn't seemed too close but was their cabin still standing? Property could easily be destroyed during intense fighting. Would they have a home to return to once the armies left?

She had to go and find out. Hopefully, no one would notice her while fighting continued across the valley.

A finger tapped on her shoulder. She jumped and stifled a scream. "Jay! You scared me to death."

"Sorry, Carrie." Jay's green eyes held an apology. "I thought you heard me behind you."

She put her hands on her hips. "Now, why would I hear you behind me when I asked you to wait?"

Cannons blasted across the valley, reverberating in her ears. The blasts added to the sound of hundreds of muskets.

Blond hair fell across Jay's forehead as the heavy artillery claimed his attention. "Those cannons are going off down toward the Tennessee River. Looks like the Yankees are attacking Missionary

Ridge. I heard them cheering this morning up on the mountain and down in the valley, too. I'll bet that means the northerners won yesterday."

Hundreds of blue-jacketed Union soldiers ran across Lookout Valley toward the rifle pits at the base of Missionary Ridge, guarded by the Confederate Army. "I reckon the fighting's moved over there. It's been going on for hours."

"I've been listening to it, too." Jay stared across the valley as smoke from the ridge showed the Confederates firing on Union soldiers from the rifle pit. "You think that means the soldiers will be leaving Lookout Mountain?"

Carrie focused troubled eyes, so like her brother's, on the battle, wishing she could protect him from further bad news. "There's no telling the plans of these armies. There was a heap of fighting yesterday. Looks like the northerners won. That probably means the Yankees will be here a while longer."

Confederate soldiers in gray or butternut leaped from the rifle pits. As the Northern Army overran the rifle pit, the southerners climbed the steep grade of Missionary Ridge to join up with other Confederate soldiers. Once they began to arrive on top, the soldiers on the ridge shot down toward the Union soldiers who had no place to hide in the rifle pits. Mesmerized, Carrie and Jay watched as hundreds of Union soldiers climbed the steep sides of Missionary Ridge while Confederate soldiers shot at them. Carrie's stomach twisted in knots as one man dropped his rifle before tumbling backward. Had she watched a man lose his life? Her heart plummeted at the possibility.

"Come on. While they're busy across the valley, let's see if our cabin's still standing." She tucked a few wisps of blonde hair behind her ears that had escaped from her customary style, a single braid that almost reached her waist.

Leading the way up the path, she attempted to stay behind the brush as much as possible, knowing movement on the mountain could attract someone's attention. Last night's rain clung to some of the branches, wetting her plain brown cloak as she brushed against the foliage. She shivered in the cold breeze as they skirted around boulders.

It wasn't long before signs of the recent deluge of soldiers passing through became apparent. A few hundred yards beyond their property, trampled underbrush and young trees bent over at the base showed the hurry with which soldiers climbed the often steep grade. Part of the battle must have been fought less than a mile from her home.

When they were within a hundred yards of the cabin, she heard a faint cry.

"Did you hear something?" Unable to pinpoint the source, her eyes darted from side to side.

"Nothing but a thousand musket shots—and those cannons rocking the whole valley." Jay's eyes remained riveted on the fighting.

"Help! Help me, please." A man's raspy cry came from further up the mountain.

"Someone's hurt!" Jay scrambled up the slope toward the voice.

"Careful, Jay! It could be a Yankee." With the sure-footed steps of those accustomed to steep climbs, Carrie followed him closely.

"Hey, Mister! Could you say something again? We can't find you." Jay didn't seem at all frightened as he searched the leaf-covered ground beneath the trees.

"I'm here. To your right." The voice sounded closer.

The siblings followed the raspy voice and stopped at the side of a seriously wounded soldier. Mud covered the young soldier's bloodstained coat. A knapsack and uncorked canteen lay at his side. A rubber blanket covered half his tall frame.

"Do you have any water?" Brown hair fell across his forehead, almost touching one blue eye.

Carrie knelt beside him grudgingly. "Jay, go fetch some water."

His eyes filled with excitement, Jay picked up the empty canteen and the cork lying beside it before running toward the well outside the cabin.

She stared at the man's guarded face, wondering if she could trust him. "Which side do you fight for? I can't tell what color your coat is underneath all that mud."

Intense blue eyes searched hers warily. "Would you help me if I said I'm a Union soldier?"

She'd suspected as much. Jumping to her feet, she turned her back on him. Southern cannons had never threatened her life the way Northern shells had, chasing them into hiding.

"My wounds finally stopped bleeding, but I won't last out here in this cold too long. Last night's rain gave me a good soaking." His voice, hoarse with thirst, pleaded with her.

She turned to face him. In spite of the scruffy appearance of a few days' growth of whiskers, he appeared to be a gentleman. His brown hair touched his shoulders, so his beard wasn't all that needed cutting. Neither of these detracted from his looks. With only a blanket as protection from the elements, the handsome young man probably wouldn't survive another night in this cold November weather.

He reached his left hand toward her. "Would you walk away and let me die because I fight for the North?"

Shame filled her. Thrusting away the terrifying memories of the August day when Union soldiers shot cannons into Chattanooga while the townspeople prayed at church for the Confederacy, she kneeled beside him. Mama would never have walked away from a person in need, no matter what they'd done. "You've been shot?"

He nodded. "My upper arm burns like fire." At the sound of running footsteps, he touched his rifle.

She placed her hand over his. "It's just my little brother, Jay."

He kept his gaze riveted toward the sound until Jay bounded into sight.

"I found another canteen like this one about a month ago." Jay pulled the cork out and gave the canteen to Carrie.

Her gaze strayed to the prone soldier. "Can you sit up?"

Determination lit his eyes. "If you get me started."

She slid her arm under his shoulders and gently eased him to a sitting position. She brought the canteen to his lips. He drained it dry.

Carrie watched the soldier's gaze shift to Missionary Ridge and turned curiously. Intense fighting took place on top of the ridge. The sound of a thousand muskets mingled with cannon blasts that reverberated through the valley. Carrie shivered at the sights and sounds of a war her father had never wanted. She looked back at the wounded soldier and found no signs of triumphant gloating.

The man put the cork on the canteen and slung the strap over his left shoulder. "I'm much obliged to both of you. My name's Adam Hendricks, U. S. Army, Ninety-ninth Ohio regiment." He grimaced in pain as his wounded arm shifted. "I prayed all day for God to save me." He winked at Jay. "I wasn't sure He could hear me over the gunfire."

Jay's jaw dropped as he stared at the soldier. "Mister, God can hear the smallest whisper. Why, you don't even have to pray out loud for Him to know what you're saying. Ain't that right, Carrie?"

"That's right, Jay." She ruffled his blond hair, thankful for the reminder. Knowing what she had to do, her gaze returned to the soldier. "Mr. Hendricks, my name is Carrie Bishop. This is my brother, Jay. We can take you to shelter, but we won't be able to carry you. It's about half a mile away."

"If I can lean on you, I'll walk as far as I'm able." With his good hand, he tried to push himself up but failed.

Carrie and Jay exchanged a look when they realized it would be a rough walk back to the cave for all of them. Carrie moved to the soldier's injured side. Putting her arm around his waist, she couldn't prevent jarring his arm. He bit his lip but didn't complain. With Jay supporting his left side, they lifted him to his feet. He was almost a foot taller than Carrie, but very thin.

"I'm much obliged." His legs shook for a moment, and he closed his eyes. "Jay, if you say one of those silent prayers for me, I think I can make it. And please call me Adam."

"I will, Adam."

Leaning on the siblings, he took a step. "You must be praying, Jay."

"I am, but you gotta remember to thank Him for answering."

He took another step. "Thank you, Lord." His right arm hung uselessly at his side.

"Pardon me." Carrie halted as his arm hit her back. "If you put your arm around my shoulder, it'd be easier to walk." Her face flamed, realizing her words might sound flirtatious.

Color flooded his pale face. "Sounds like a good idea, but I can't control my arm. It won't listen to me right now. Would you mind?"

He seemed as embarrassed as she felt. It somehow made her feel better. "Not at all." She gently picked up his arm to rest on her shoulder.

Even though his lips clamped shut, a gasp escaped him.

"I'm sorry. Can you manage?" It occurred to her the bullet might have broken a bone.

He smiled at her. "Don't you worry about it. I've been through worse than this and lived."

"You have?"

At the spellbound look on Jay's face, Adam's teasing grin seemed to come with great effort as he winced in pain. "Well, maybe I'm stretching the truth a bit on that one, Jay." His step faltered. "Looks like I'm going to need to concentrate on my walking for a few minutes."

· CHAPTER TWO ·

nion tents filled the valley surrounding Chattanooga and were easily visible from this side of Lookout Mountain. The battle raged on across the valley. Carrie prayed it would keep the attention of Union soldiers on the fighting and not on their slow progress around the mountain. By the time they made it to the cave, Adam was barely conscious. The last fifty yards he dragged his feet, his head down and eyes closed. Exhausted from bearing the brunt of his weight, Carrie was almost too beat to dread what Aunt Lavinia would say when they brought a Yankee into the hiding place.

Perhaps if they placed Adam on a pallet in the front room of the cave, Aunt Lavinia wouldn't even realize he was there. After all, she hadn't been out of bed more than a few minutes a day since they moved to the cave. Carrie would have to find a way to keep her talkative brother from mentioning Adam.

As they neared the entrance, Carrie whispered, "Jay, we'll keep Adam in the front room. Don't tell Aunt Lavinia he's here."

His brow furrowed. "Why not?"

"She won't want us to help him."

His eyes widened, but he agreed to keep silent. Adam didn't respond to the whispered conversation. With his head already bowed, they were able to maneuver him through the low entrance. When Jay released him to gather blankets for his pallet, Adam collapsed on the floor. Their dog, Star, barked a welcome and came over from his place beside the fire to lick Adam's fingers.

"Carrie, is that you?" From the adjoining room, Aunt Lavinia sounded both worried and annoyed.

"Yes, Aunt Lavinia, we're back." She removed her bloodstained cloak before hurrying to the next room to soothe her aunt. "Supper should be ready in a little while."

"Well, I should hope so." At fifty, her illness made her seem older than her years as she picked up the quilting square beside her on the bed. "You were gone long enough. The battle must be further away. The vibration from cannons doesn't seem as strong today. I'll just bet our army showed those Yankees who's boss, and they're running back home. Did you gather enough firewood?"

Carrie managed not to gasp, having forgotten all about her original excuse for leaving their shelter that afternoon. "I ... I'll have to go back for a couple of loads after I build up the fire in here."

"Well, hurry up. The fire's getting pretty low. I don't need to get any sicker." She coughed as if to remind her niece of her lung complaint.

Since Carrie heard about it in some form or another every day, no reminder was necessary.

Their cave didn't go back very far into the mountain, but it had three high-ceiling rooms. Aunt Lavinia and Carrie slept in the middle room, which was the largest. A neighbor helped them bring a wagonload of furniture to the cave before his family headed south or they wouldn't be nearly as comfortable. He had tried to convince Carrie and her family to flee with them, but her aunt wouldn't hear of it. No Yankee was going to chase her out of town. Besides, her health would have made any trip a hardship, so they had moved to the cave. Aunt Lavinia's narrow bed had been deemed a necessity and had been selected over a table. The mattresses from the other beds had also been moved with blankets, clothing, and all the food they owned.

The back room was used as the stable for the chickens and cows to guard against anyone passing by hearing them from outside the cave. The chickens sometimes wandered into the bedroom, pecking the ground in search of fallen grain. The rooster crowed throughout the day and night, often waking Carrie from a sound sleep. Jay bedded down in the front room with their collie mix dog, Star, so named for the white star on the top of his head.

Carrie quickly threw small twigs on the burning embers within the circle of stones in the middle of the chilly room. She must attend to Adam's wound soon, although what she could do beyond providing a clean bandage remained a mystery. She had never removed a bullet in all her twenty years—or even seen it done. Hopefully, clean bandages, nourishing broths, and protection from the elements would be enough. The poor man had seemed all done in when he collapsed on the ground moments ago.

Once the fire crackled with warmth, she placed a log on it and left through the six-foot wide passage to the main room. Jay had already removed the unconscious soldier's coat and blouse. Dried blood and grime surrounded the torn flesh of his upper arm. At least she could remove the dirt.

She dropped to her knees beside him. "Fetch me some clean cloths and a bucket of water."

Jay quickly returned with the items. He watched Carrie wash the arm as gently as possible. Adam groaned when her cloth found another wound. She lifted his arm to investigate. "There are two wounds, one on the top and one near the back of his arm, higher than the other by at least three inches. He must have taken two bullets."

Jay inspected it with her. "Maybe it was just one bullet that came out the other side."

Puzzled, Carrie's gaze fell on Adam's blue coat where Jay had tossed it earlier. Picking it up, she examined the sleeve. There were two holes corresponding with his wounds, but no bullets. "Since I don't know anything about removing a bullet, I reckon one bullet is the best we can hope for."

After Carrie bandaged the wounds, Jay helped her wash his chest and back so they could put one of Papa's old nightshirts on him. Papa was off in Virginia with General Lee's army, so he probably wouldn't mind. She couldn't help noticing that the skin stretched over Adam's ribs, as if he hadn't eaten a good meal in a while. She didn't have any older brothers—just Jay—so she felt a tinge of embarrassment to be performing such an intimate service for a handsome stranger.

Jay suggested cutting off the right sleeve of the nightshirt so the bandage could be changed easily. Although Carrie didn't like the idea of cutting up Papa's clothes, it would make caring for Adam easier, so she agreed.

When they finished, they covered him in the rubber blanket they'd found with him. "Why, it's a poncho, Carrie. There's an opening for his head."

She nodded. "I guess that comes in handy during long marches in the rain. I'll dry out the wet blanket from his knapsack by the fire. Lying out in the cold rain after getting shot didn't do him any good. Aunt Lavinia finished another quilt last week. Put that over him, too, while I start supper. Then step outside. If you don't see any soldiers, gather up firewood."

Carrie made up the fire within the circle of stones in the middle of the front room before making potato soup from the dried potatoes she'd put on to soak earlier in the day.

Jay came back with an armload of branches before leaving for another.

Wondering whether Adam still slept from exhaustion or something worse, Carrie crept to his side. His flushed face felt hot to her cold hand. The poor man burned with fever, probably from the drenching he'd received from last evening's rain. She soaked a rag in cold water and wiped his hot face.

He stirred and opened his eyes. "Miss Bishop?"

She dropped the cloth back in the water to make it cold again. "You can call me Carrie. Everyone does."

"Where are we?" His blue eyes searched the room before returning to her face.

"This is a cave near my family's property. We've been here since your army took over Chattanooga in September." She tried to keep bitterness out of her voice. It was more than an inconvenience to stay here. They'd lived in fear for months.

"Most folks leave when soldiers make camp in their town." His gaze held hers.

"We would have left if we could. My aunt is too sick to travel." Aunt Lavinia's condition had worsened after the Confederate army made their camp in Chattanooga during the hot days of summer. "After our horse went missing one night, I knew our cows and chickens would be next. So far no one has found this place."

"I'm glad of that." He closed his eyes and rubbed his forehead. "Could I trouble you for another drink of water?"

She gave him a dipper of cold water, which he drank as if parched. "I'm making soup for supper. It'll be ready shortly."

"Much obliged to you." His voice sounded stronger after he drank his fill.

His eyes remained closed, so she put the cold cloth on his forehead.

"Carrie!"

Adam's eyes opened at the sound of her aunt's high-pitched voice.

"That's Aunt Lavinia. Don't let her see you."

He moved the blanket aside and started to push himself up.

Carrie stopped him with a hand on his shoulder. "She's bedridden with consumption and hasn't been out of that room in days. You should be safe if you stay in this front room. Just keep your voice low and try not to make much noise."

He relaxed back onto the blanket, but his expression remained wary. "I don't mean to cause you trouble."

"It's no trouble." She stood and picked up a candleholder. "I'd better go see what she wants."

· CHAPTER THREE ·

*T*hrough the glow of a circle of candlelight, Adam watched Carrie leave through an entrance to the back of the cave. He wondered why she had decided to help him when she clearly didn't trust him. Some soldier had stolen her horse, which troubled him. What he didn't know was which side had done it. Perhaps she suspected Union soldiers, since she had been tempted to leave him to die on the mountain.

He wondered about Aunt Lavinia, whom he hadn't laid eyes on yet. She must hold a grudge against Yankees. Had she lost a relative to the war? There'd been too much bloodshed on both sides. Perhaps Carrie had hesitated to help him because of her aunt's attitude. He'd have to keep his wits about him in case the woman acted on her anger.

This main room was about twenty feet wide and obviously functioned as the kitchen area with barrels, dishes, and a few pots. Two candleholders with lit candles and a glowing fire provided the only light. A mattress next to the wall showed where Jay likely slept. Were there any other members of the family? Should he be concerned about anyone else's anger or hatred toward a Union soldier?

He sniffed appreciatively. Could that smell be potato soup? After living on increasingly diminished rations for several weeks, he still didn't have his fill. He remembered that wonderful day a couple of weeks ago when three river steamers came around Moccasin Point loaded with food. He had stood on the bank of the Tennessee River with other hungry soldiers who cheered them on. He drew five days of rations and ate two days' worth in one meal.

His eyelids drooped. His arm felt more comfortable, but the pain bothered him more than he cared to admit. Thanks to a night spent on the cold, wet mountain, he had a fever. When the second bullet found its mark, he'd been intent on getting to the rear of the army and finding medical attention. Obviously he had lost his way in the darkness. He remembered seeing the eclipse of the moon. Loud cheers from further up the mountain and from the valley early that morning brought a smile to his face. The Union had been victorious yesterday. He yelled for help, but no one heard. Hugh would have been looking for him along with others, but Adam had wandered too far from his regiment. He had prayed all day they would return and find him for he didn't know how long he could survive under those conditions. Carrie and Jay had saved his life. He hoped to find a way to repay their kindness.

A wet sticky bandage told him the wound bled again. The walk to the cave had almost done him in. Each step had jarred his arm, making the half-mile journey pure torture. His eyelids drooped as weakness overcame him. Hopefully, Aunt Lavinia wouldn't choose this moment to leave her chambers because he couldn't stay awake any longer.

As he fell asleep, his thoughts turned to the green-eyed Carrie with hair the color of ripened wheat. Would she save him from enemies inside this shelter? Or must he flee before his strength returned?

Carrie stirred the soup before dipping out a bowl for her aunt. Thankfully, Adam slept on, but Jay hadn't returned from fetching another load of wood. She fretted over him. Although it would be fully dark soon, her little brother felt at home on the mountain. It would soon be time to milk the cows, one of Jay's chores. Under normal circumstances, she wouldn't worry, but the fighting on Missionary Ridge had slackened. From inside the cave, she couldn't hear any cannons and didn't know if shots were still being fired. Soldiers from either side could return to Lookout Mountain at any time. Then they would be trapped inside during the day unless the soldiers chose another part of the huge mountain to occupy. With her view of Chattanooga and the whole valley, she knew this area to be a probable location.

Aunt Lavinia usually fell asleep soon after supper. She'd had a long coughing spell a little while ago which exhausted her. It would be best to get some nourishment into her before she slept.

Carrie heaved a heartfelt sigh as she took the filled wooden bowl into the bedroom. Aunt Lavinia hadn't always been so bitter. In the days before the war, she'd been the one who took care of the cooking and other chores while Carrie tended the garden and the animals. Papa had taken a job in Chattanooga building locomotive engines after Mama died of pneumonia back in 1857. Everything had changed after that.

Aunt Lavinia, a childless widow and Papa's sister, had come to live with them to help raise Jay, then only three. The burden of raising a family had weighed on Papa, and his teasing manner vanished. When whispers of the coming war reached him, he hadn't been in favor of secession. He hadn't been in favor of slavery, either, and they'd never owned any. Carrie had been certain he leaned on the side of the North until Confederate soldiers came to their home and insisted he join their army. Carrie had been frightened at the way they held the loaded muskets. The hard look on the leader's face had only softened when Papa agreed to go with them.

Soon after that, Aunt Lavinia started losing weight and going to bed with the chickens. Once the doctor told her that she suffered from tuberculosis, all the fight to recover had gone out of her. He recommended bed rest, poultices, and a spoonful of his own personal remedy. To Carrie, it smelled like the wine served at a neighbor's home, but Aunt Lavinia took it obediently several times a day.

When Carrie entered the shadowy bedroom, Aunt Lavinia's eyes were closed, her sewing forgotten at her side. "Aunt Lavinia? I've brought soup for you."

"Thanks, child." Her thin face seemed paler than normal, but it could be the dim lighting. "The candle's burning low. Can you light another?" One of the two candles they kept burning in this room at all times sat on her aunt's bedside table. It had less than an inch left to the wick.

"I'll help you sit up first." Carrie put the bowl on the table and assisted her aunt to sit with her shoulders against the wooden headboard. "How are you feeling now?"

"Weak." Aunt Lavinia rubbed her temples before reaching for the steaming soup. "My head aches. I'll need some of Dr. Townsend's elixir after supper."

"All right." Carrie fetched a candle from a box in the back of the room. "We've been going through more candles living in this cave, but this supply should see us through the winter."

"Even if we must stay here?" Her aunt ate another spoonful of soup.

"Yes." Carrie hoped they'd be leaving before long because Aunt Lavinia's health had declined since they moved. She kept that observation to herself. The cows bellowed from the back room, reminding her of the passing time. Where was Jay?

"The vibrations have stopped. Is the battle over?"

Carrie sat on the edge of the bed. "I don't know. The fighting was over on Missionary Ridge today."

Aunt Lavinia gave Carrie a half-filled bowl. "That was good, Carrie. You're turning into a right good cook."

She stared at the contents, chagrined at her aunt's poor appetite. Always petite like Carrie, Aunt Lavinia had lost even more weight since they fled their home. "Don't you want any more?"

"No." She sank down into the bed and pulled the blankets up to her shoulders. "Them soldiers done took what's left of my appetite. The way they run us out of Chattanooga when their cannons fired on us—while we sat in church praying for the Confederacy!—was plumb shameful. And now we've been run out of our home and into this cave where it's always cold. It's all that blamed Lincoln's fault."

With a Union soldier sleeping some forty feet from where she lay, the gray-haired woman's words jolted her. "I don't think President Lincoln wanted the war."

"He ain't my president!" Aunt Lavinia's dark eyes blazed in anger. "Don't you dare call him that, Carrie Elizabeth! If it weren't for him, my brother would still have a job in Chattanooga and not be off fighting a war he's too old for."

With her attitude about the Union's president, she wouldn't react well to Carrie aiding a wounded Yankee soldier. Carrie tried not to let the anger affect her, but hearing the same complaints time without end made it difficult to maintain a positive outlook. The bitterness that dwelt in this room was like an insidious poison seeping into her soul.

"When I watched that meteor flash across the sky and break in two before the election, I knew it was a bad sign. And I was right." Her anger apparently drained the last of her energy. Her words trailed off.

Carrie remembered that day, too. During one of the political speeches of the 1860 presidential campaign, a meteor streaked across the sky. When it broke into two parts, some people saw it as a sign that the country would split. Aunt Lavinia was one of them. Carrie sighed and stood. "Get some rest now, Aunt Lavinia. I'll bring the medicine in later."

"Thank you, child." She closed her eyes.

Jay came in with another bundle of wood as Carrie exited the shadowy chamber. He dropped the load next to the growing stack near the opening of the cave.

Carrie breathed a sigh of relief. "That's enough wood for today. Thanks, Jay. What took so long?"

Adam stirred but didn't awaken.

A sheepish look crossed Jay's face. "I might have sat down to watch the muskets flash on Missionary Ridge. I think the Union won, Carrie. I saw an awful lot of movement in the valley and on top of the ridge. Men wearing blue shouted and cheered. There's a bunch of them over there."

She shivered at the news as if a cold draft had entered with Jay. That news wouldn't soothe her aunt's mood at all. "Since you don't know for certain who won, let's not mention it to Aunt Lavinia. She won't like it."

Jay stared down at Adam. "Yeah, she hates Yankees." The tall man lay very still on his pallet as Jay's green eyes looked up at her trustfully. "Do we hate Yankees, too, Carrie?"

· CHAPTER FOUR ·

dam waited tensely for Carrie's answer. If she hated him, he'd best seize the first opportunity to escape.

"The Bible says not to hate people, Jay. We hate the war."

Her voice sounded further away, so he peeked through slit eyes. She had turned to the table against the wall. He couldn't see what she was doing or her expression.

"I like Adam." The little boy's honesty felt refreshing.

He closed his eyes tightly as booted footsteps approached.

"He's heavy, though."

Adam clamped his mouth shut to suppress a laugh. Jay was a good kid.

"Wash up. We'll eat and then wake up Adam. He'll need nourishment to get better."

After sounds of splashing water from the other side of the room ended, brother and sister sat around the fire. Carrie asked the blessing, including a prayer for her papa off fighting the war with General Lee in Virginia, her aunt's health, and for Adam. The simple heartfelt prayer moved him. He decided to continue pretending to sleep to learn more about his host family. Another peek showed the siblings faced the cave entrance, carefully covered with brush.

"Be careful not to wake Aunt Lavinia when you go through to milk the cows. She's not feeling well."

Blond hair fell across Jay's forehead as he bent over the bowl. "She's worse. Ain't she?" He looked at his sister with fear in his eyes.

Carrie swallowed hard. "I'm not a doctor. She hasn't been seen by Dr. Townsend since everybody cleared out. It's hard to tell."

"There's still plenty of her medicine, right?"

She put her hand on his shoulder and squeezed. "Four more bottles. He gave us all he had before leaving. She'll be fine until he returns to town."

Jay's brow furrowed in thought. "But Carrie, if the Union army stays in Chattanooga, will the doctor come back?"

Her face turned pale. "I hadn't thought of that. We'll just pray people return home before the medicine runs out." She sighed. "It's time for our lives to get back to normal."

He put his bowl on the ground in front of him. "What happens to us if Papa doesn't come back and Aunt Lavinia dies?"

Carrie's eyes glistened with tears for just a moment before she jumped up to retrieve the water bucket and dipper. She returned to her place in front of the fire before answering. "We'll pray that neither of those things happens."

"But we prayed the war wouldn't start either, and it did. We prayed Papa wouldn't have to choose a side to fight on, and he did. We prayed that Union soldiers would stay away from our mountain." He rested his elbows on his knees and leaned his face on his hands. "I reckon we're not too good at praying."

Carrie scooted over and put her arm around him. "Mama used to say that sometimes God says no to something we want really bad. She said that's the hardest time to trust Him, but it matters most then. When times get hard, trust God harder."

"Is He still with us? Even in this cave?" The boy's green eyes shone with hope and trust.

"Especially in this cave." A couple of cows bellowed from further inside the cave. "Guess we'd better get to our evening chores. I'll wake up Adam in a few minutes."

Jay left the room. Carrie took their dishes to a long table that lined the rocky wall. Adam's heart ached as her shoulders shook silently, glad for the glimpse of what the past couple of years had been for them. Their mother must have been quite a woman to have instilled such faith in them. His faith had taken a beating after losing too many comrades, good men who deserved to live and return to their families. Perhaps he should have fought harder to trust God even when it hurt.

If he couldn't help her, at least he could distract her. Careful not to dislodge his throbbing arm, he moved his legs so that his shoes scraped against the rough stone.

Her body stilled instantly. "I'll be right there."

Retrieving a handkerchief from the pocket of her plain brown dress, she swiped at her cheeks before turning around. "You must be hungry."

Since his last meal had been before noon yesterday, the understatement coaxed a reluctant smile. "Yes, Ma'am."

She brought a steaming bowl of soup over and knelt beside him. "Can you sit up to eat?"

He tried to push himself upright with his good arm, but couldn't manage it. "Sorry. Guess I'm weak as a baby right now." He gestured to his wounded arm with a nod. "Much obliged for the bandages."

"My pleasure." She rolled up a blanket and placed it under his pillow to prop up his head. "Just rest and regain your strength. I'll feed you." She gave him a bite of delicious soup. "I don't know anything about removing bullets. There are two wounds. Either you've got two bullets in your arm or it went all the way through."

He grinned. "I got hit early in the day. I couldn't reload as quickly but could still fire my weapon. The second bullet came after dark. It was my fault. I should have been more alert to the sound of their pickets approaching." Her answering smile made his heart skip a beat. She sure was pretty. "And you've already done plenty for me."

The wounded arm didn't affect his appetite. He ate every last bite. "There's a little more if you want it."

Soldiers learned early not to turn down home-cooked food. "I'd be much obliged."

"My pleasure." His appetite seemed to please her for a smile lit her face as she returned to his side with a steaming bowl of soup.

"It's very tasty. I haven't had soup this good since I left home." He concentrated on eating the second helping, but it became an effort. "Thank you kindly for the meal." To his frustration, weakness overcame him. Since when had eating become a chore?

"You rest now." She put a cool hand on his burning forehead. "I have some powders for that fever. Don't fall asleep until I fetch them."

"I'll try."

She hurried away. Despite his best efforts, his eyelids closed in sleep.

For the next three days, all Adam did was eat and sleep. He fed himself with his left hand unless the meal consisted of soup. Feeding himself soup with his left hand defeated him so far. He took care of any personal needs, striving for as much independence as possible. The fever continued, causing Carrie to wonder if he'd caught pneumonia in the rain. It could also be the bullets in his arm. It seemed pointless to probe the arm searching for them when she could do nothing to remove them.

After searching the trunk for Dover's powder to lower his fever, she realized the medicine had been left back in the cabin. As she prepared a poultice for her aunt to ease her cough, she wondered if a poultice would help Adam's arm. Deciding it couldn't hurt, she made a poultice with flaxseed meal and applied it to the wounds. The muscles in his face relaxed as it brought relief, prompting her to apply poultices two or three times daily.

She couldn't deny that Adam was growing on her. Whenever she changed his bandages or applied a poultice, he always had a kind word or a teasing comment for her. Though she had plenty to do, waiting on him became a pleasure. She couldn't help liking him.

After Jay saw Union soldiers in Chattanooga the day after the battle, Carrie wouldn't allow him outside. The little boy remained restless, cooped up inside the cave. For that matter, Star didn't handle the forced inactivity any better. The family pet took a shine to Adam and had been sleeping on the floor beside him. When awake, Adam talked to Jay like an older brother. He made a fuss over Jay's dog, which could account for Star's strong liking for the stranger.

Carrie had listened to a conversation between Adam and Jay yesterday that revealed more of the soldier's background.

After finding out that Adam lived on a farm a few miles outside of Lima, Ohio, Jay had asked about his family.

Though his face had been flushed with fever, Adam propped himself up against the wall to answer Jay's questions.

"My father died seven years ago, about a month after my fifteenth birthday." Sadness shadowed his blue eyes. "I always knew I'd take over the farm one day, but I thought I'd be married by then." He met Carrie's gaze as she scrubbed mud from his uniform. "Since I was the oldest, a lot of responsibility fell on me. I wasn't ready for it. I just wanted my father back."

Jay bowed his head. "My ma died when I was three. I can't hardly remember her."

Star licked his hand.

Adam's eyes filled with compassion as he placed a hand on Jay's shoulder. "I sure am sorry to hear that. She sounds like a wonderful lady."

Jay looked up at him. "That's when Aunt Lavinia came to live with us. She took care of me and Carrie while Pa worked."

Adam's gaze went from Jay to Carrie. "So you don't have any other brothers or sisters?"

"No. Just Carrie." Jay stroked Star's head. "Aunt Lavinia was nice back then."

Appalled that her brother could say such a thing to someone outside the family, Carrie felt she had to explain. "She doesn't feel well, Jay. Lots of folks get cranky when they're sick. We've talked about this. Remember?"

He nodded. "It gets harder to remember when I can't go outside and play."

Carrie couldn't help sympathizing. Nine-year-olds needed to run, climb trees, and explore. He couldn't do those things with the war on their doorstep. Hoping to distract him, she decided to discover more about the soldier who somehow tugged at her heart with his refusal to complain of his pain. "So you're the oldest in your family, Adam?"

"I have three sisters and a brother. My brother, Allen, is the youngest."

Jay perked up. "How old is he?"

"Allen is fifteen." Adam frowned. "He's running the farm now with my sisters. I made him promise not to join the army until he's at least sixteen."

"When's his birthday?"

Adam tried to smile. "Next September. Maybe this will all be over by then."

"Amen." Carrie wasn't aware she spoke aloud until she felt Adam's intense blue gaze. "We've had our fill of war."

"Me, too." Adam's expression held compassion and sorrow.

All the fight went out of her at his quiet admission. He didn't want this war any more than she did. It seemed a strange conversation to hold with a soldier who fought on the opposite side as her father. Carrie didn't know what to say, but felt any lingering animosity toward him slip away. She began to see him with different eyes, as someone she wanted to get to know.

"Our pa's fighting in Virginia." Jay's troubled look tore at Carrie's heart.

"Is he? Your pa must be a very brave man."

A look of pride brought a smile to Jay's face. "He is. He's not always fighting though. He mostly works on train engines and the railroads. Is that brave too?"

Adam grinned. "You better believe it. That's an important job."

"Yeah, that's what Carrie says."

The satisfied look on her brother's face comforted Carrie.

"Your big sister is pretty smart." Adam ruffled Jay's blond hair. "You should listen to her."

It relieved Carrie when Adam turned the conversation away from the war. When Adam rubbed his forehead for the second time with his good hand, she wished she hadn't forgotten the headache powders at the cabin.

Confederate soldiers had gone through the cabin shortly after the men took up residence on Lookout Mountain. Anything of value was already in the cave, but the medicine had been overlooked. It was kept on a shelf in the root cellar with Aunt Lavinia's other medicine. Could it still be there?

She changed Adam's bandages daily. After his clothes had been mended and washed, they were hidden in the bottom of one of the barrels with sacks of cornmeal on top in case her aunt felt up to walking into the main room. All signs of his allegiance to the North had been hidden. If Adam healed quickly, they might be able to keep his presence a secret.

Although she wasn't a doctor, his injury didn't look any better. This morning ugly purple bruises surrounded the swollen skin.

Adam had watched her face. "How does it look?"

She sighed. "It's bruised. I think I'll try cleaning it again."

When she brought over a bowl of water and lye soap, Adam pretended to cringe. "You're not planning to wash out my mouth with soap, are you? No one's done that since I was about Jay's age."

She couldn't help laughing, and he grinned. "This is for your arm. The smaller wound is scabbing over, but the other one is still open.

It can't hurt, can it?"

"I doubt it will hurt you much." Still teasing, he made a face as if scared. "It'll probably sting some for me."

She laughed again. Working quickly, she bathed the whole area and rinsed it. When she was done, she smiled at him. "Let's hope for the best. If some dirt had made its way inside the wound, soap can't hurt. I don't know how to do anything else."

His face was a little pale, but he managed to grin. "Reckon it was worth a try. Once."

"All right. We won't do that again. Hopefully it will close up now."

"I'll start praying now." He spoke with mock seriousness.

She laughed again and returned to her chores.

After supper that evening as Carrie washed the dishes, Jay brought in two buckets of milk from the back of the cave and poured it into a three-foot urn.

She peaked into the urn. "That's not as much milk as when they stayed in the barn."

Jay shrugged. "Reckon they need to get out into the fresh air as much as anybody else." He crossed the room to sit beside Adam. "What are you thinking about, Adam? Your arm hurt?"

Adam grinned and forced himself to sit up and lean against the wall. "No, I'm all right. I was just thinking about a girl back home."

Alarmed to hear of another girl, Carrie's gaze flew to the soldier. "What's her name?"

Adam rubbed his injured forearm. "Sarah."

"Is she your girl?"

Carrie bent over so that wisps of blond hair hid her gaze from Adam as she tried to appear too busy to listen.

"She didn't want to be a soldier's girl."

Jay folded him arms. "That's dumb. Being a soldier is the best job."

Adam grinned and ruffled Jay's hair. "I think so, too."

Star joined them and they began to fuss over the dog.

Carrie regretted not hearing a bit more about the girl back home. Was she waiting for him? It didn't sound like it.

Did that bother Adam?

For no reason she could understand, her spirits plummeted. She listened carefully to the conversation across the dimly lit room, but Sarah's name didn't come up again.

His actions remained those of a gentleman. Always polite and grateful for the slightest service, he had altered her attitude about Union soldiers. His kindness to Jay didn't go unnoticed either. As she normally preferred clean-shaven men, she tried to imagine him without the beard. Nothing could mask his intense blue eyes which seemed to pierce all the way to her soul. She couldn't deny feeling drawn to him.

When Adam showed no improvement the following morning, she made up her mind to visit the cabin. The medicine might not reduce the fever or pain, but she felt compelled to try. Even if he did fight on the opposite side as her father, she didn't want him to die. She now knew him to be a good man. She would do everything in her power to save him.

· CHAPTER FIVE ·

arrie waited until Aunt Lavinia ate supper and settled to sleep before leaving the shelter. Jay wanted to come with her, but she convinced him to stay and feed Adam the remaining vegetable soup. Adam watched her leave with a concerned expression. Star came along after being admonished not to bark.

The cold air caused her to shiver until the brisk climb toward the cabin warmed her. A winding wagon road passed about fifty feet from her home to the foot of the mountain. It didn't go near the cave. Southern troops had camped about a mile from her home during the autumn. Had the soldiers been further away, she might have been able to stay there. She sighed. Now that the Union army had defeated the Southerners, the Northerners were likely to stay in the area for a while. Her family would take shelter in the cave for a while longer.

Full darkness hadn't fallen yet, and she knew movement could be seen across the valley, should anyone be watching, so she walked behind trees and underbrush whenever possible. His nose to the ground, Star followed her silently.

She kept her guard up, always searching for signs that soldiers had returned. Rustling leaves made her jump, but the squirrel circled the oak tree harmlessly. So far, so good. Maybe she and Jay should make a few trips to the well near their home with some buckets. The water barrel was still over half full, but there was no way to know the army's plans. The soldiers could return any day. One of the food barrels was empty now. It wouldn't hurt to use it for extra water. They'd go tonight after she searched the cabin for anything they could use.

Their home had been built on level ground with about two acres for her garden. The cows had a fenced pasture not far from the garden, as there were too many steep embankments and cliffs to be certain of the animals' safety. The barn with an adjacent corral for their horses had several missing rails since the last time she'd been here about a month ago. The Confederates had undoubtedly helped themselves to some firewood. A smokehouse, henhouse, and a few storage buildings made for a comfortable home, whenever they could return to living there.

How she longed for the not-so-distant days when they had felt like a family! Aunt Lavinia's constant complaints wore Carrie out faster than their living conditions could. With no letters from Papa since early summer, they didn't know how he fared. She knew that letters couldn't get through easily with Union occupation of Chattanooga, so she refused to consider the possibility he might have been wounded.

She was glad to leave her gloomy thoughts behind upon reaching the cabin. Muddy footprints showed others had been there. One of the chairs left behind lay in pieces on the floor, but the dining table was merely dusty.

She lit the candle from her pocket and lifted the lid to the cellar. Climbing down the ladder, she crossed to the shelf where the medicine had been stored. Somehow the soldiers had missed the packets of powders on the bottom shelf. She snatched them up gratefully. If she'd left any of Aunt Lavinia's elixir behind, the bottles were gone now. In fact, the rest of the shelves were barren. There had been fabric and old clothing down here along with a supply of lye soap. Why hadn't she thrown those items into the loaded wagon with the rest of their possessions? No use crying over what couldn't be changed.

Leaving the house, she went to the barn where three stacks of baled hay had been stored. No! It couldn't be true.

Nothing remained. She rubbed her hand across suddenly throbbing temples. This loss hurt. They didn't have enough feed for the cows back at the cave to last the winter. What could she do now? And which army deserved the blame? Both had been near enough to find the barn.

Picking up one of the unbroken chairs, she carried it back to the cave. At least the soldiers wouldn't get this chair.

The moon lit the way for several trips to the well outside the cabin. It was closer than the creek at the base of the mountain. Hundreds of campfires surrounded Chattanooga in the distance. Star accompanied Carrie and Jay as filled buckets sloshed water on them in the cold. It was far too dangerous in the darkness to take the shorter mountain trail that led perilously close to steep drop offs.

Thoroughly exhausted, she led the way into the cave on the last trip and almost dropped the precious cargo. In her cotton nightgown, Aunt Lavinia held a piece of firewood threateningly as she stood a few feet from where Adam lay with his gaze fastened on her.

"Aunt Lavinia! What are you doing?" Carrie set the buckets down carefully and began to approach the wild-eyed woman on the opposite side of the room.

"Carrie, he's a Union soldier!" She shook the six-inch thick piece of timber at Adam. "Why is he here?"

"We found him on the mountain. The other soldiers had gone." Her heart thudding, she glanced at Adam as he rose to his knees unaided. Watching both of them warily, he pushed himself to his feet with his uninjured hand as if ready to bolt. "He's been shot. He would have died on the mountain."

The gray-haired woman glared at Adam. "It would have been good riddance if he had. One less Yankee to trouble us. You should have left him there."

Carrie didn't believe her aunt would hit Adam with the sturdy piece of wood, but the older woman had surprised her before. She prayed silently for his safety. He didn't need any more wounds. "Aunt Lavinia, I know you don't mean that. Why, Mama would turn over in her grave if we had left him to die."

"Your mother always did have a soft spot for those who suffered."

Carrie took another step forward. "Yes, she did. I know you do, too, deep down inside. Please don't hurt this soldier who has been every inch a gentleman since he came."

"His name's Adam, Aunt Lavinia." Jay's earnest green eyes pleaded with her from Adam's side. "He won't hurt us, not even when he gets better. He likes us. Even Star."

"Adam Hendricks, United States Army." He gave a respectful nod to the older woman. "Pleased to make your acquaintance, Ma'am."

"Don't you try to cotton up to me, Yankee!" Her eyes blazed. "I've heard how you've been destroying towns and burning mills so folks can't feed their children. You ought to be ashamed!"

Her words filled Carrie with fear for the soldier who had befriended her and Jay. Nothing must happen to him.

"If you want me to go, I'll leave now." His tone remained respectful as hatred charged the atmosphere.

"No! He can't leave. He's not strong enough, Aunt Lavinia." Carrie rushed to her aunt's side and impulsively clutched her arm. "Please don't force him to go. He'll die before he reaches the army camps in Chattanooga."

"That ain't no concern of ours." Aunt Lavinia finally turned her angry gaze to Carrie.

"Yes, it is." Carrie usually agreed with her aunt to keep the peace, but couldn't afford to do that this time. Adam's life depended on it. "He's a good man, Aunt Lavinia."

She glanced suspiciously at Adam. "I'll bet he's killed some of our soldiers."

"If he did, it's only because of the war. Both sides have lost too many." Heart thudding, she stared at the log still raised toward Adam. "Please, let me do what I can to save his life. There's been too much bloodshed. Let's not add to it."

"Please, Aunt Lavinia?" Jay shook as he added his plea.

The wood fell with a thud. "And he's gone as soon as he's better."

"When he's strong enough to cross the valley." Carrie held her breath.

Aunt Lavinia patted Carrie's hand. "Help me back to bed, child. I'm all done in."

"Of course." Allowing the older woman to lean on her, she stole a relieved look at Adam. His grave expression didn't change as his eyes searched hers. Perhaps he still felt in danger. "I'll be back in a few minutes. Jay, empty the water into the barrel and give Adam a drink."

· CHAPTER SIX ·

fter watching Carrie leave with her aunt Adam slumped onto his pallet. He had believed the older woman meant to bludgeon him where he lay when she first entered the room with the piece of firewood. The crazed look in her eyes had scared him even more than his first battle. When Carrie entered, sloshing water on her dress, it seemed God had sent her in answer to one of those silent prayers Jay had mentioned.

What would have happened if she hadn't returned at that moment? His strength had waned to the point he might have been unable to avoid the blows. Would he have been facing his Maker at the tender age of twenty-two?

Suddenly shivering, whether in reaction to the bitter scene or fever, he pulled the blankets over him. One thing of which he was certain— he wouldn't fall asleep again next time Carrie and Jay left the cave.

Jay brought him a dipper of water and knelt beside him. "Sorry about Aunt Lavinia. She wasn't like this before she got sick."

Adam took one look at the boy's miserable face and knew the ugliness had affected all of them. "Don't you worry about it, Jay. Sometimes people aren't themselves when they feel poorly."

"She's got consumption. Dr. Townsend said the medicine will make her feel better." Jay sat and leaned against the wall. "He never said she'd get better."

This little boy had seen hard times. He wouldn't be fooled by trite sayings. If Adam was any judge, his aunt was not at all well. He took a long drink and gave the dipper back. "I'm just a soldier, Jay. I don't know about such things, but I can tell you one thing. Your sister will take good care of you. You need to listen to her better."

He frowned and then nodded. "I know. Carrie used to let me outside to play or walk the cows home or fetch water. She hardly ever says yes to anything anymore. I'm tired of being cooped up in this cave."

Adam listened intently, wanting to ease the young boy's restlessness, if possible. "I certainly can understand that. I've been here four, maybe five days?"

"Five days. You came on Wednesday. It's Sunday night. Tomorrow's the last day of November."

"Five days, then. It's hard on us men to be inside that long, isn't it?"

Jay rested his elbows on his knees and leaned his chin on his fists. "I'll say."

"If these were normal times, she'd be fine with you and Star roaming the mountain around here, right? As long as you were careful?"

He nodded.

"Unfortunately, it could be dangerous out there. We fought on this mountain a few days ago. You weren't outside then, were you?"

Jay shook his head. "I wanted to watch, but Carrie wouldn't let me."

"That's because you have a smart sister. Bullets fly in all directions during battles. They ricochet off trees and boulders. You have a few of those around here, don't you?" Since great boulders jutted out in many areas, Jay would understand this argument.

He nodded. "Lots of them."

"I got shot during the fight, but I know the Union won. I listened to another battle the next day over on Missionary Ridge. I don't know what happened. Either way, soldiers are likely to come back and camp on the mountain."

"It's a big mountain." A certain amount of pride lit Jay's eyes.

44

"Most of it is in Georgia, but we live in Tennessee. Maybe they won't be anywhere near us."

"Maybe not. If they are close, you don't want them finding this cave, do you?"

"They'll steal our food and our animals. They already took our horse."

Adam sighed, regretful of this family's suffering. They lived in fear. "Your sister mentioned that. You're right to hide the cows and chickens. Fresh eggs, milk, and butter will keep you fed a long time."

"Carrie told me the soldiers took the rest of the hay out of our barn. She doesn't know how we'll feed the cows when the hay runs out." Jay's green eyes grew huge with worry.

Adam closed his eyes in regret at the crippling news for the brother and sister who had shown such kindness. He hoped it was the work of the Rebel Army. "How much do you have here?"

"Oh, there's enough for a couple of months, maybe longer. We carried over as much as the back room would hold when we moved in."

Adam leaned back on the pillow, exhaustion claiming him again. There had to be something he could do for this family. When he rejoined his regiment, he'd come up with some way to help them. If he recovered. He grew weaker instead of stronger with each passing day. Those slugs of lead in his arm must be taking a toll on him.

"Adam?"

Jay's voice seemed to come from far away. "Yes?"

"I'm going to be a doctor one day. Then I can help folks like you and Aunt Lavinia. Just thought you'd like to know."

Pride filled him at the heart and courage in this young boy. Adam forced a response before sleep claimed him. "Glad to hear it. You'll make a fine doctor."

Carrie emerged from the bedroom after a long talk with her aunt. Finding out Adam had been with them since Wednesday further

45

angered the older woman. Carrie had listened to her aunt's tirade before appealing to the compassionate nature that must still survive in her aunt.

Jay had fallen asleep next to Adam with Star in between them. She tapped her brother's shoulder and got him settled on his own mattress before retrieving a clean cloth and a bowl of water. Kneeling beside Adam, she touched his burning forehead. The headache powders hadn't done any good yet. He wouldn't get any more medicine tonight unless he woke up.

Hoping to cool the fever, she washed his face with cold water. She wondered if Aunt Lavinia would really have killed him. What if she and Jay hadn't arrived? She felt protective of the soldier but didn't understand why. The thought of someone hurting him frightened yet angered her at the same time. Did his weakened state bring out her protective spirit for a man she had met less than a week ago? Or did her heart whisper a deeper reason?

She dropped the cloth back into the water and stepped outside into the darkness, needing solitude. Covering her face with her hands, she leaned against the stony boulder near the entrance. She couldn't be falling in love with a Union solder—not with Papa fighting on the side of the South in Virginia. What would he think?

She sank to the freezing ground, thankful a dense fog hid her from view. These feelings must be a result of working so hard to save his life. She'd heard of the bond that sometimes formed between a caregiver and patient. That must be it. She'd recover soon enough once he returned to one of those campfires flickering in the valley.

She didn't know what else to do for him. His condition had not improved. The headache powders didn't alleviate the pain or fever. He couldn't die. He just couldn't. She bowed her head and prayed for his complete recovery. She also asked for wisdom to know how to help him.

When the cold drove her back inside, he was awake.

"Did the pain wake you?"

He nodded. "I thought you were sleeping."

"I feel restless tonight." She sat beside him. "Would it help to talk a few minutes?"

"I'd like that, but it's late. You're tired."

The concern in his eyes for her felt good. It had been a long time since someone watched over her. "I won't be able to sleep either. How long have you been a soldier?"

With his good hand, he managed to get into a sitting position and leaned against the wall. "I mustered into the army last August. In 1862. Since I was the head of the family, my mother didn't want me to go when the war began. Finally it seemed wrong not to go."

"My pa was thirty-nine when the war started." Carrie sat facing him on the ground a couple of feet away. "I thought he was too old to fight. Two Confederate soldiers came to the house in early May of '61. They carried muskets and wanted Papa to sign up that day. I'm not certain Papa would have chosen to fight for the South. He never believed in slavery."

Adam raised his eyebrows.

"I can understand your surprise, especially after the way I acted when we met." She looked away. "I'm sorry about that. Mama would have been ashamed of me."

"It's been hard since your pa left."

"You have no idea." Suddenly it felt important that he understand. "Aunt Lavinia got sick shortly after he left. I wrote to Papa about her illness but never told him how much her health had declined. I'm so worried about him. He's now forty-one. No matter what those men said, I think he's too old to be a soldier."

He nodded. "We've got folks in their forties, too. And boys in their early teens. That's what scares me so much about my brother. He wanted to join when I did. I had a hard time convincing him to stay behind and look after our mother and sisters."

Carrie understood his concern for his brother. Didn't she worry about Jay every day? "He's so young."

"And life can change in an instant — especially during a battle."

They stared at each other. They'd never been this serious with one another or talked about something so important.

Suddenly afraid to share more, Carrie stood up slowly. "Do you think you can sleep now?"

He nodded, his intense gaze never leaving hers.

"Well, good night then. Send Jay in to get me if you need anything." She tried to smile but felt herself trembling with emotion.

"I will. Good night, Carrie."

She started to walk away.

"Carrie?"

"Yes?" She turned back to look at him.

"I'm glad I met you." There was no teasing light in his eyes now. He meant it.

Her breath caught in her throat. "Me, too."

The atmosphere became charged with emotion. This time she teased him to break the tension. "So I could learn some new nursing skills."

He smiled. "Aw. Happy to know I'm good for something."

She returned his smile. "Sleep well, Adam."

As she got into bed, she realized the smile was still on her face.

· CHAPTER SEVEN ·

arrie endured her aunt's complaints about Adam as best she could for the next few days. Aunt Lavinia insisted on Carrie's help to walk to the front room. Every day she sat in a chair facing Adam. Carrie didn't know if her aunt intended to protect her family or remind the soldier of her presence. Either way, all felt relieved when Aunt Lavinia returned to her sickbed after an hour or so.

It had to make Adam uncomfortable and concern him, but he didn't complain. In fact, he went in and out of sleep several times a day. He was friendly with her, but didn't talk often. Carrie's worry for him increased as she realized his condition was worsening.

She changed his bandage daily and applied the poultices. The bruised, torn flesh didn't show much improvement. She went back to using plain water to wash the arm, but it didn't change the appearance of the open wound.

If he wasn't busy with chores, Jay sat beside her as she tended Adam. No matter how gruesome the sight appeared to her, Jay paid close attention.

Realizing both Jay and Star were fidgety, Carrie sent her brother out to replenish the firewood on Friday, December 4th. When her aunt retreated to bed after breakfast for a nap, Carrie took the opportunity to pray for Adam again as the soldier slept restlessly. Her ideas had run out, and still Adam showed no signs of improvement. In fact, he grew weaker. One of the wounds remained open. The bullets must be lodged inside the arm somewhere. Aunt Lavinia couldn't remove them, even if she could be persuaded to help a Yankee. Jay couldn't do it. All their close neighbors had fled. Of those who remained further up the mountain, would any possess the skill to remove a bullet?

Thoughts of the army tents surrounding Chattanooga came unbidden. The army had surgeons. But no, it was at least a two or three-mile walk to get to the closest camp. She couldn't take Adam to them. He couldn't walk such a distance, and they had no horse. If she brought them to the cave, their food could be stolen along with the livestock. They would starve. She couldn't do that to her family.

Adam had been shot on November twenty-fourth. The bullets had now been in his arm ten days. They must be removed. What could she do? How could she save Adam's life and not risk the livelihood of her family?

"Carrie!" Jay burst into the cave as she fried bacon to accompany the cornbread. "Soldiers are back on the mountain."

Frustrated, she put her hands on her hips. Would they never be able to return to their home? "Where did you see them?"

Excitement lit his green eyes. "On the plateau. Up near Summertown. I saw soldiers waving flags at the hotel. Tents, too."

"Summertown?" Wealthy folks used the village, located in the high altitudes about two miles from their home, as a summer resort. "I think everyone who lived there left already."

"Yeah, I didn't see anyone I knew. Just a passel of soldiers."

Her heart leaped to her throat as she removed the skillet from the edge of the fire. "Just how close did you get to them?"

He shrugged. "Not real close. I hid behind bushes when I saw a bunch of tents. Star didn't growl or anything, not even when a squirrel ran up the chestnut tree next to us. I heard them talking about fixing the road."

"Jay Bishop, that's too close! They were Union soldiers?" Although Adam's eyes remained closed, something in his tense posture showed he wasn't sleeping.

Jay nodded. "Just like Adam. I like Yankees now, Carrie. Don't you?"

She flushed. "At least one of them. But someone stole our horse."

"It wasn't Adam."

She liked Adam, too, maybe even more than Jay did. She'd been taking extra care with her appearance the past few days, pinning her braid up in a more sophisticated style that she hoped pleased the soldier. "I know. Why don't you wake him while I take a plate into Aunt Lavinia?" She poured a glass of milk and went into the large, middle room.

"What's all the excitement?" The older woman didn't sit up when Carrie entered. "Do I need to go in there?"

"No, Aunt Lavinia, please rest." She hesitated, not wanting to get her aunt stirred up again. "Jay saw soldiers on the plateau around the hotel in Summertown."

"Yankees?" Her pale eyes filled with fear and loathing.

Carrie nodded reluctantly. "There are enough tall trees, jutting ledges, and boulders to hide us from their view. We'll have to be careful not to make noise to draw their attention when we go outside. Do you want me to feed you?"

"Can't believe they had the nerve to come back." Aunt Lavinia rubbed her temples. "No, just leave it on the table. I'll eat when my headache eases some."

Carrie patted her arm before returning to the front room. Jay ate next to Adam on the floor. "Where's Adam's plate?"

"He ain't that hungry."

Carrie put her hands on her hips and gave Adam her best 'big sister' look. It always worked on Jay. "Not that hungry? After I went to all the trouble of baking cornbread?" He simply had to eat to maintain his strength.

He looked a little ashamed. "Bacon smells good, too."

"That's more like it." She put several slices of bacon on a plate next to a generous wedge of cornbread and brought it to him. "Do you feel like sitting up?"

He closed his eyes as if to muster his strength. "Jay, old boy, think you can give me a hand?"

Jay hunkered over and put an arm around Adam's shoulders. He eased the grown man into a sitting position with gentleness beyond his years.

"Thanks, Jay." He reached for the plate. "Did I ever say thank you for all the wonderful meals?" He smiled at Carrie.

Her heart melted. He really was a good man. "At least a dozen times. Now, eat everything on your plate."

He chuckled and winked at Jay. "Yes, Ma'am." Still grinning, he asked, "Have you ever considered joining the army?"

She frowned, surprised by the question. "Why would you ask such a thing?"

"Because I think you'd make a fine officer." He started to chuckle again, but winced when laughter jarred the wounded arm.

"Are you all right? Is it worse?" Instantly she fell on her knees at his side, eyes intent on his face.

He quickly masked his pain with a forced smile. "Jay, can you check on the chickens? I want to speak privately to your sister."

The boy carried his empty plate to one of the barrel lids Carrie used as a table top before heading to the back of the cave.

Adam put down his plate to hold her hand with his good hand. "Carrie, I'm not getting better. I don't want to die in front of your brother. Can you get to the soldiers up on the mountain? Go to the Union camp. Tell them that I'm with the Ninety-Ninth Ohio. They'll come for me."

Tears sprang to her eyes. He couldn't die. "No, you're not going to die on us, Adam Hendricks! We've lost too much already."

He squeezed her hand tighter. "Would losing me be such a great loss?"

She couldn't meet that intense gaze and certainly couldn't speak of her private feelings when she didn't know how he felt. "Of course. I wouldn't want to see anyone die."

He looked down at their clasped hands. "Of course not. You're a compassionate person." He released her and ate a piece of bacon.

She slowly crossed the room to get her food. Tears continued to fall silently. She bowed her head and prayed silently. *"Lord, please show me the way. And don't let Adam die. Please don't let Adam die."*

Jay came back into the room. "Was that enough time?"

Adam met her gaze across the room. "Yes, thank you, Jay."

"Why are you crying, Carrie?" Her little brother placed a gentle hand on her arm.

She closed her eyes to ask silently for strength. Then she looked at Jay. "Because I have a difficult task ahead of me. Will you help?"

· CHAPTER EIGHT ·

"*'ll do anything.* Please don't cry."

The trust in Jay's expression as he looked at his sister warmed Adam's soul. She had done a good job raising him.

"I know you will." She put her hands on Jay's shoulders and looked at him intently. "Adam needs a doctor. Since his army is camped further up the mountain, I'll go and let them know he's here."

"To our hideout?" His few freckles stood out on a suddenly pale face.

A determined light in her eyes, she gave him a brief hug. "That's where I need your help. If we work together, we can carry some of our food back to our cabin. The soldiers have already been there. I doubt they'll search it again."

"But what about the rest of it? And our cows and chickens? If the soldiers go back into the cave, they'll find them. Cows make too much noise to hide them. And what if the rooster crows? Then we won't have any milk or eggs or butter."

Carrie patted his arm distractedly. "I don't know what they'll do."

"And what will Aunt Lavinia say?"

Glancing toward the bedroom with a sigh, she shrugged. "If more Union soldiers are coming here, I should warn her first." She began to walk in that direction.

"Wait!" Adam couldn't jeopardize their safety. He knew all about livestock disappearing when rations ran low. If soldiers knew where an excess of food could be found, they were likely to try to buy it or even take it. Why hadn't he considered that possibility? His brain must be befuddled with pain. After all this family had done for him, he wouldn't put them in that position. "Take me to your cabin instead."

She looked at him speculatively. "Can you make it that far?"

"Yes." He answered as firmly as possible, but honestly didn't know the answer. If he collapsed along the way, it would be better than exposing their hidden shelter. His wounds would likely prove fatal anyway. His death would be difficult for this little family. If things had been different, maybe he could have courted the beautiful Carrie with her mixture of feisty gentleness, but it was best not to dwell on what could never be.

Jay tugged on his sister's sleeve as she stared at Adam contemplatively. "Carrie, did you hear? We can take him to the cabin instead."

Her sad gaze finally shifted to her brother. "I heard him, Jay. I don't believe he can walk that far."

Still wearing his army trousers and Mr. Bishop's old nightshirt, Adam pushed back the blankets and pushed himself up to his knees with his good hand. The wounded arm hung limp at his side. He suspected the bullet had broken a bone. "Of course I can. I'll be fine if I lean on someone."

"See, Carrie? I'm strong. I'll help."

She seemed even more burdened to be given the alternative as different emotions registered on her face. Adam could almost feel the indecision, fear, and helplessness from across the room. "Let me speak with Aunt Lavinia."

When she left the room, Jay came over to him.

"Jay, if you could help me over to that chair, I'll put my old brogans on. I'll need those shoes on the cold mountain trail."

Jay helped him rise to his feet. The boy seemed to understand Adam's need to gather his strength before shuffling to the high-backed chair five feet away. "It's right nippy. I'll take an armload of wood up to the cabin before we go. The cabin's freezing."

After Adam sank into the chair, Jay retrieved the rest of the soldier's clothing from the bottom of a barrel. He helped Adam slip on his blouse, coat, and shoes. "I'd best be on my way so I can hurry back. I'll take Star with me."

"Be careful out there."

He watched the boy head out with all the wood he could hold in his arms and another loaded sack of kindling over his shoulder.

Adam touched his throbbing arm. The wet bandage, now hidden under his coat, could mean an infection or his wound had started bleeding again. Despite nourishing meals, he'd felt himself weakening the past few days. Carrie had done all she could do for him.

God had certainly watched over him in guiding him to such a caring family. Of course, their aunt hadn't shown much compassion, but could he really blame her? With no doctor to tend her, the consumption must be growing worse. This chilly cave dwelling couldn't be very healthy for her. Through the course of the war, this family had been shot at and gone into hiding through fear of losing their possessions. The man of the home had left to fight for the Southern cause many miles from here. They'd lost at least one horse and a generous supply of hay. Who knew what else they'd endured?

And now, a Union soldier would likely die in their hiding place. How could he add to their troubles by allowing the United States Army to discover the entrance to their cave? Carrie grew sweeter and more compassionate every day. Even though the decision tore her up inside, she would go to the army camp and bring back a surgeon for him. She'd put her family at risk. He loved her for it but couldn't allow it.

He loved her? Where had that thought come from? She could order him around like the best sergeant taking him through the drills and then in the next moment gently bind his wound.

He groaned aloud as the sure knowledge came. His love for her didn't change anything. If he thought he could live … but, no, the pain and swelling in his arm convinced him otherwise. He didn't need a surgeon to realize it. He'd seen too much during his time in the army.

No, he'd find the strength to walk to the cabin or die in the attempt. This family wouldn't have to sacrifice any more for him after he made what could be his last journey.

An hour later, Carrie gritted her teeth as Adam slumped further, leaning even more of his weight on her. His eyes had been closed for the last ten minutes, but his legs continued forward as if he were on a long march. Gray clouds blocked the sun. A biting wind blew her cloak open. Adam's arm around her shoulder felt as if it weighed at least a hundred pounds.

Wisps of blond hair had escaped from the single braid that had been securely pinned to the crown of her head that morning. Relief filled her as the cabin came into sight at last. The normal ten-minute walk had stretched to over thirty minutes. Jay had scampered ahead to build up the fire, leaving her supporting most of Adam's weight.

Aunt Lavinia had been all for moving Adam to the cabin. She couldn't wait to get the Yankee out of the front room. She hadn't been as thrilled with the idea of her niece visiting the army camp, but on this point Carrie remained firm. It provided the only possibility of saving Adam's life. This afternoon, Jay would help carry supplies to them and then remain with Aunt Lavinia. Adam must wait in solitude while Carrie climbed the mountain.

Her fretful aunt refused to be left alone in the cave. Star remained to protect her while they were gone. Jay would stay at the cave to care for the livestock and his aunt. It wasn't the best arrangement, but Carrie couldn't come up with a better plan in light of Aunt Lavinia's nerves.

A few feet from the door, Adam tripped over a jutting tree root. They both hit the ground hard. Adam groaned as he landed on the injured arm and lost consciousness. Winded and exhausted, Carrie laid next to him long enough to catch her breath. Then, dusty and covered with dead leaves, she pushed to her feet. She tried to lift him by his shoulders. It didn't work as he only budged a few inches.

"Adam!" No response. "Adam, please. You must help me. I can't lift you."

He didn't awaken. No amount of tugging moved his unconscious form more than a couple of inches toward the cabin.

She sank to her knees. The door was only eight feet from where Adam lay. It felt more like a mile. "Jay! Come out here and help me!"

The cabin door opened, and Jay rushed outside without a coat. "Is he dead?" Fear washed over his face.

Carrie shook her head. "He fell on his injured arm and passed out. Help me get him inside."

She moved to Adam's right side, careful of his injury as she placed her hands on his shoulders. Jay took a strong hold of Adam's left arm. The good food Adam had eaten in the time he'd been with them must have helped him put on some weight. Using their combined strength, they couldn't budge him even a foot closer.

Carrie gave another mighty tug and fell on her backside, panting.

"He's too heavy." Ever practical, Jay moved to sit beside her. "He's gonna have to help us or stay where he's at."

Carrie silently acknowledged the truth. Her strength had almost been spent by half-carrying Adam along the trail. She didn't have enough left to get him inside, but how could they awaken him? Even with all the tugging, the poor man remained unconscious.

Her eyes went to his wounded arm. He'd fallen on it and then lost consciousness. If she poked the wound, would he awaken?

With nothing to lose, she crawled over to him. She tried tapping on his arm, but he merely stirred. Mouth set firmly, she doubled her small hand into a fist and struck the bandage.

Adam groaned and opened his eyes. His lips compressed.

Carrie leaned over him. "Adam! We're almost to the cabin. I'm sorry about punching you, but we couldn't get you inside any other way. Please help us. Can you get up and walk inside?"

Although pain clouded his eyes, he managed to grin. "You punched me to awaken me? That was a right good wallop as my buddies would say."

Carrie could have wept, so great was her relief at his teasing. "Try to get on your feet. Jay made a nice, warm fire inside."

Adam winked at Jay. "Good man. Thanks, Jay."

He struggled to his feet with support from both of them. Within a couple of minutes, he laid on Papa's old mattress in front of the fireplace that Jay had prepared for him. Carrie managed to give him a dipper of water before he fell into a troubled sleep clutching his injured arm.

· CHAPTER NINE ·

arrie and Jay made a trip back to the cave for blankets and food. Then he reluctantly returned to the cave to care for Aunt Lavinia after a strong warning from his sister to remain there.

Carrie watched him trudge back to the shelter from the window, hoping he heeded her request this time. Generally obedient, he hated the confinement of the cave. He loved the outdoors. Being cooped up inside weighed heavily on him, but his safety depended upon it. The army surgeon wouldn't come alone. Yankees would soon be milling around on their property. If Jay left the shelter when soldiers were near, they could easily find the cave entrance.

She sighed and turned toward Adam, still sleeping near the fireplace. The main room had warmed up nicely with a crackling fire. The warmth after a long walk would likely keep Adam comfortable and cozy for a couple of hours. She'd best make the trek up the mountain before darkness settled in.

After carrying the water bucket and dipper to Adam's side, she sliced a wedge of cornbread. She placed the plate next to the water within his easy reach.

Kneeling at his side, she stared at him. The pain on his face didn't ease as he slept. The walk had exhausted the wounded soldier. They had almost dragged him those last few steps. He hadn't complained once, but he hadn't felt like leaving the cave. She had to admire his compassion and courage. He had walked this difficult path so the troops wouldn't find her shelter. Her livestock and food should now be safe. He had saved them.

Now it was her turn. She touched his rough whiskers with her fingertips. His skin felt too warm. Worried about the fever, she realized the powders that might relieve it were back at the cave. It couldn't be helped now. Undoubtedly, the doctor would have whatever Adam required.

This would likely be her last time alone with him. She would miss him when they took him away. He had become very dear to her. If things had been different … *"Lord, please save Adam's life. Send a surgeon who knows how to help him. Don't let him die, Lord. Oh, please don't let him die."*

Thankfully, her whispered prayer didn't awaken Adam.

It was past time to go. She stood. After putting on her warm cloak, she gave him a final lingering glance.

She stepped out into the cold. The path to the mountain road was barely wide enough for a wagon in a couple of places where underbrush had started to grow again from lack of use. Following the road up the mountain should lead to army troops. This afternoon she walked openly, wanting to be seen. Setting a brisk pace as the wind increased on the gloomy day, she climbed the mountain, praying for Adam's life and the safety of her family.

Despite her trepidation at meeting Union soldiers, she enjoyed her first freedom since artillery shells had destroyed parts of Chattanooga in August. Today she didn't hide her presence from watchful eyes. Instead, she wanted to be found.

About an hour later, she heard men's voices. Before she could register the direction of the sound, six soldiers joined her on the road. Their blue coats showed traces of mud with a few tears. The oldest might be in his early thirties while the youngest had no need to shave yet. They carried knapsacks, wooden canteens, and rifles with the business end pointed to the ground.

They all stared at her. Knowing that most of the residents all over the mountain had fled, she understood their surprise. It didn't lessen the fear that overtook her.

One of the older ones stepped forward. He touched his cap respectfully. "I'm Sergeant Dan Young. Pardon our surprise, Miss. We haven't seen anyone but soldiers up here. Where are you headed?"

His courteous manner slowed her heartbeat to a more normal rhythm, but her hands shook visibly. She tucked them under her cloak. "I'm Carrie Bishop. I need a doctor."

He exchanged a glance with the man next to him.

"It's … it's not for me. It's for you. I mean, at least it's for one of your soldiers. Adam Hendricks was shot during the battle last week. He's with the Ninety-Ninth Ohio."

His eyes widened. They all straightened, seeming more alert.

"My bro—er, that is, I found him last Wednesday." Her glance slid nervously from face to face, hoping they would help. "I've been caring for him ever since. I've done all I can do. He needs doctoring."

They all looked at the sergeant. "He's been missing," said the only clean-shaven man.

"Hugh Bellamy was looking for him after the battle. I figured he got captured," said another.

"Reckon we can carry him up to the surgeon."

"No!" Remembering his fever, Carrie didn't believe Adam could survive another rugged trek so soon. "Please, can you bring the surgeon to him? He's doing poorly."

"Guess we'd better inform Lieutenant Otto," Sergeant Young said. "Baker, come with me. The rest of you return to picket duty."

The thin officer's gaze returned to Carrie as four men disappeared into the brush. "This way, Miss Bishop."

She followed the men until dozens of tents appeared. Sergeant Young led the way to one of the larger tents. Asking her to wait outside with Private Baker, he stepped inside.

Wind whipped around her skirt, causing her to shiver. Not much taller than her, Private Baker appeared the bashful sort. He scuffed his muddy shoes in the dirt to avoid looking at her.

Afraid that all the trouble to get to the camp might come to naught, she pulled her cloak tighter against her. How long would this conversation take? She'd been gone well over an hour already. Adam would awaken and need her.

A man wearing a dark blue coat with stripes on the sleeve emerged moments later. Of average height with a graying beard, he nodded respectfully. "Miss Bishop, I'm Lieutenant Otto. I hear you've been caring for one of our men."

"Yes, Adam Hendricks is at my family's cabin." His watchful gaze didn't change, and she didn't know if he would agree to send a doctor. "Please, he's very ill. He's been shot twice. I think the bullets are still inside. He's feverish. Even though I kept the wounds clean, they don't look good to me."

"There are surgeons here. We'll send an ambulance. We appreciate your care for him." He turned to the sergeant.

Carrie heard him give orders for an ambulance with horror. Adam wouldn't survive a wagon ride on this rocky, steep road. She grabbed the lieutenant's arm. "Please, sir, send the doctor to Adam. The bullets should be removed and then he'll need to recover his strength."

His expression showed that compassion fought the necessity of hard decisions. "Miss, we have sick and wounded here that demand attention. A hospital has been set up. He'll be in good hands."

Why wouldn't he listen to her? Her eyes pleaded with him. "You don't understand. I fear he won't survive the hardship of a trip today. Please send a surgeon to him. The doctor won't have to stay after he removes the bullets. If he leaves instructions, I'll follow them."

He frowned, but appeared to be wavering.

"Please, sir. You can't afford to lose another good man if it can be helped."

He stared at her for a second before chuckling. "Miss Bishop, Adam's a lucky fellow to have found such a champion." He rubbed his whiskered chin. "Sergeant, see if any of the surgeons can be spared until morning."

Sergeant Young grinned at her before he strode away.

Relief flooded over Carrie. "Oh, thank you, Lieutenant Otto. It's awfully good of you."

"Happy to be of service, little lady." He started to reenter the tent, but turned back. "One word of caution. The surgeon will make the decision as to when Adam can be moved. If that's in the morning, so be it."

Carrie dared not argue. "Of course. I only have Adam's well-being in mind."

"And I must consider dozens of men. You may wait inside for the ambulance if you wish." He gestured toward his tent.

Carrie didn't know if it would be proper to accept his hospitality, but couldn't relax anyway. "No, thank you most kindly. I'll wait here for the surgeon."

He nodded respectfully and went inside.

Fifteen minutes went by as she waited in the cold with the bashful soldier. She began to pace to restore feeling to her feet. She hadn't properly prepared for the biting wind of the higher altitude.

As dusk approached on the dismal afternoon, fog descended over the mountain. Carrie began to worry that it would be fully dark before they reached the cabin. The fog would only add to the danger of descending the winding, steep grade. Another ten minutes passed before a four-wheeled vehicle came into sight. With canvas sides and a roof, it bore a yellow flag with a red "H."

Sergeant Young gestured to the soldier on the ground. "Here, Baker, take the reins." He waited until Baker held the reins before jumping down. "Miss Bishop, Dr. Hastings agreed to go to Adam. Please ride inside with him." He led the way to the back, which was completely open. "You'll be a bit warmer in here, Ma'am. We'll take the road down. Let us know when we're getting close."

Dr. Hastings, a graying man of about forty, stood slightly and lifted his hat to acknowledge an introduction by Sergeant Young. A large leather bag rested on the bunk near him. The sergeant unfolded one of the lower bunks from the side of the vehicle for her before joining Baker up front.

Carrie perched on the wooden bench nervously, hoping the doctor didn't find it an imposition to help her. Then she lifted her chin. This trip wasn't for her, but for one of this army's soldiers. She wouldn't apologize for the inconvenience.

Dr. Hastings asked several questions about Adam, his wounds, and his condition before settling into silence. The gruff man seemed weary and soon fell asleep sitting up, despite the bumpy ride.

· CHAPTER TEN ·

ense fog made the mountain road more dangerous. Baker slowed the horses to a walk until the fog dissipated for the last mile of the journey. The smell of burning wood along with wisps of smoke from the chimney led the soldiers to Carrie's home, making it unnecessary to supply directions. When they arrived, Carrie didn't wait for anyone to assist her from the ambulance. She raced inside, closely followed by Sergeant Young.

Face flushed with fever, Adam opened his eyes as they entered. Carrie dropped to her knees at his side. "Adam, I've brought Dr. Hastings for you."

He managed a smile as the door closed behind the doctor.

The older man knelt awkwardly on the floor. "Soldier, you've caused a lot of trouble today. This young woman insisted I come to you."

Chagrin mingled with gratitude on Adam's face as he glanced from Dr. Hastings to Carrie. "I regret the inconvenience, Dr. Hastings."

A twinkle appeared in the doctor's eyes as he winked. "Glad to do it, son. Let's see about getting you fixed up and back to your duties."

"Yes, sir."

The doctor supported Adam's back to lift him to a seated position. Adam greeted the sergeant, who he seemed to know. With the sergeant's assistance, they removed Adam's outer clothing until coming to the nightshirt with a sleeve cut away. The doctor examined the swollen, bruised arm for several minutes, probing and prodding while Adam clenched his teeth.

Carrie picked up the plate of untouched food she'd left at Adam's side and moved the bucket back to the stove that Papa bought shortly before Mama died. She waited tensely, her gaze fixed on Adam's closed eyes.

"I believe one of the bullets lodged on the outside of the arm." Adam put his fingers on a spot near the elbow.

Dr. Hastings probed the area. "Yes, that one shouldn't be a problem to remove." He continued to examine the entire arm.

Baker entered as the doctor came to a decision.

He rose to his feet, glancing at Carrie. Walking toward one of the two bedrooms, he stopped at the threshold. "Those bullets must be removed. We'll use the table for the operation. Gentlemen, please carry the table in here. Build a fire in the heat stove before moving the patient in here."

The soldiers went about following his instructions.

Carrie saw Adam watching the doctor open his leather bag and shifted her gaze. Among the items were bandages, scissors, and medicine bottles. Dr. Hastings took out a fine wooden box with a fancy design on top. She felt the blood drain from her face at the collection of small to large ebony handled knives nestled inside the deceptively beautiful box. She covered her mouth to keep from screaming at the sight of a saw sharp enough to go through a bone.

She had heard of amputations being performed on soldiers, but she'd never met anyone who lost a limb in such a way. Is that what Dr. Hastings planned to do? Must Adam lose his arm?

Before she could react, Adam spoke up. "Will you be able to save my arm, Dr. Hastings?"

The doctor didn't even glance at Adam's ashen face. "I can try, son."

"Doctor?" When the man continued to search through the medicine bottles, Adam raised his voice. "Dr. Hastings, please try to remove the bullets and any splintered bones only."

Distracted with preparations, Dr. Hastings glanced over as the soldiers carried the table from the room. "Of course, son."

Devastated by the dismissive response, Adam closed his eyes. Reaching over with his good left hand, he moved his fingers up his right arm as if feeling it for the last time.

Carrie dropped to her knees at Adam's side, her heart breaking for him. "Dr. Hastings, can you save his arm?"

The desperate question finally broke through the doctor's concentration with his task. He stopped his preparations to consider the couple staring at him fearfully. "I don't know, young lady." He sighed. "The bullets have been lodged inside well over a week, which presents a problem. There's certain to be fragments of bone. His fever is high. I'm not convinced it's worth the attempt."

"That's because it's not your arm!" Carrie leaped to her feet, angry that he didn't even plan to try. "Please, sir, you've come all this way. Saving his life is the most important thing, but won't you do what you can to save his arm? He's still a young man. Besides, he can't shoot a rifle with one arm, can he? Don't you need every good man you can get?"

The gruff man's bushy eyebrows almost met as he stared at her, perplexed and angry. Then he began to chuckle. "The sergeant warned me you don't quit. You're a lucky man, Adam Hendricks, to have such a guardian angel on your side. Very well, I'll do what I can." His face turned grim. "No promises. Adam, those are serious wounds, neglected far too long. If you're a praying man, I suggest you get to it. We'll begin once the fire's lit."

Carrie kneeled beside the prone man, realizing he could die. She sandwiched his left hand in hers as they stared at each other. "I'll pray with you."

He gripped her hand and closed his eyes.

They were only given a moment of silent prayer before the soldiers came for him.

Before the men reached his side, Adam placed his good hand

on her shoulder and drew her closer until their lips met. His lips clung to hers in a sweet, gentle caress.

The kiss held sadness as if at a parting. Fear swept through her as the realization struck that Adam believed this to be a final goodbye. He didn't expect to live. "You'll be fine, Adam. Dr. Hastings is an experienced surgeon." She prayed it was true.

As they lifted him, his hand slid from her shoulder. "Thanks, Carrie. For everything."

She gave him a trembling smile. "I'll have supper waiting for you." Following them to the doorway, she saw the doctor put some liquid on a cloth before the door closed in her face.

"Save him, Lord." She didn't care if anyone else heard her whispered prayer as long as God answered.

Carrie soaked dried vegetables in water before preparing vegetable soup. Undoubtedly the men would be hungry when the surgeon finished removing the bullets. The meal would stretch further with wedges of cornbread from breakfast. Unless the soldiers brought coffee with them, she'd serve water with the meal. A plentiful supply of milk and eggs should satisfy all appetites at breakfast.

Once a full kettle of soup heated on the stove, she carried bedding into the old bedroom she once shared with Aunt Lavinia, making a pallet for herself on the floor since her mattress was still in the cave. After she built a cozy fire inside the heat stove, it removed the chill from the room.

Where would the soldiers sleep? In the main room in front of the fire or in the barn? She hated to think of them sleeping in the cold barn, but it would make her feel more comfortable to have the strangers there. The surgeon would decide whether to keep Adam in Papa's old bedroom or move him to a spot near the fireplace.

Since she didn't know how to prepare for sleeping arrangements, there was little else she could do. Wandering aimlessly back to the kitchen, she stirred the soup with a long, wooden spoon. How long did it take to remove two bullets anyway?

Patience had never been her strongest virtue. The longer she waited, the more tense she became.

Baker came out of the room a few moments later. "Pardon me, Miss Bishop. The doctor's asking for a kettle of water to heat on the stove inside the surgical room. Also, he's asking to use the pitcher and bowl for …"

Carrie paled at the thought of the blood.

"What he needs." The private kept his eyes on the floor as he finished the request.

"Of course. I'll get the water. The other things should already be inside the room."

The man's cheeks flushed crimson. "We couldn't seem to find the usual items in the room."

Carrie shook her head in humiliation at the oversight. The only set was in her old bedroom, along with the chamber pot. She could visit the privy behind the house, but Adam would require this convenience. What else had she and Jay forgotten? "Please bring the items from the other bedroom while I fetch water from the well." She picked up a bucket and started for the door.

Baker reached for the bucket. "If it's all the same to you, Miss Bishop, I'll fetch the water while you gather the other items." He went outside, letting in a cold draft which caused Carrie to shiver.

She added two towels to the items requested. The simple tasks were accomplished all too soon. Carrie returned to the stove to stir the gently-bubbling soup after the soldier returned to Adam's room. The surgery had already taken a couple of hours. What could be taking so long?

Doubts began to creep inside her heart. What if Dr. Hastings didn't have enough knowledge and experience to help Adam? This seemed unlikely as the man had to be at least forty. If he had practiced medicine all these years, surely the war years would have provided the necessary experience by now.

What if the bullets couldn't be found? Would the arm be removed? Would this be enough to save Adam's life or would it further endanger him?

The door opened and Baker emerged. He tried to hide the contents of the bowl in his hand, but it was too late. Carrie paled at the sight of bloody water. Baker rushed outside with the bowl.

She crept toward the open door where Dr. Hastings bent over Adam. "How is he?"

The sergeant met her with an expression of concern, closing the door behind him so she couldn't see the patient. "I've never assisted a surgery before." He wiped his face with a big white handkerchief. "The first bullet came out easily. The other one was harder to find."

Her heart skipped a beat. "Have both bullets been removed?"

He took another swipe at his forehead. "We found two pieces. Doc Hastings is sewing him up right now. I best not say any more than that." He glanced at the stove, sniffing appreciatively. "Is that vegetable soup in that pot?"

· CHAPTER ELEVEN ·

ergeant Young carried the mattress that Adam had been using and placed it onto the bed frame in Papa's room. Then he and Baker lifted the still sleeping Adam from the table to the bed. Dr. Hastings covered him with a blanket.

"Do you have any lye soap, Miss Bishop?" The polite sergeant blocked the doorway so Carrie couldn't see inside.

"Yes. I'll get it for you." She turned her eyes away from the table as she went to the kitchen area of the main room.

The soldiers took the table outside while Carrie rummaged through a basket she'd brought from the cave. Young promptly returned.

"Here it is." She gave the sergeant the soap and a towel.

"We'll wash your furniture before bringing it back inside." He didn't look at her, alluding to the blood stains from Adam's surgery.

Carrie swallowed hard. "Thank you, Sergeant Young. I've made supper for everyone, but I only have two bowls."

"Oh, that's no problem, miss. We brought our own." He grinned as he left with the cloth and soap.

Moving slowly as if exhausted, the doctor finally emerged.

Carrie rushed to his side. "How is Adam?"

He took one of the two unbroken seats and moved it near the fire before relaxing his tired frame on it. "That's a good question. I believe all of the bullets are out, but I'm not certain. There were a couple of bone fragments. He was weak and feverish before I arrived and he's still very sick. I'm afraid we won't know for days if he'll …"

"What?" What did he imply? Horrified, she covered her face with her hands. She forced herself to ask what she most feared to hear. "He's not going to …" The words died on her lips.

His eyes filled with compassion. "He's very sick, Carrie."

She gulped at his repeated warning. "How about his arm? Did you save it?" Her heart pounded fearfully to hear the answer. Adam loved serving as a soldier.

"For now. The bullets and bone fragments have been removed. We'll just have to see if the muscles can heal."

Carrie closed her eyes briefly, praying for strength for Adam and her. "Thank you for trying to save his arm. I've made supper. You're welcome to serve yourself. The men will return with the table shortly. Remember to save some for Adam."

She went in to see Adam. His pale face scared her as he had been red and feverish when she last talked with him. His skin felt hot and dry.

Baker brought the porcelain bowl back to the bedroom and replaced it with fresh water. She bathed Adam's face and hands with the cold water. Then she retrieved a chair from the main room to sit beside Adam. As soon as he woke up, she'd give him a nice refreshing drink from the well.

She held his good hand while staring at his face. God could pull Adam through this. She'd certainly made her wishes known in her frequent prayers for him the past week.

It didn't matter what side of the war he fought on. He had to live. He must live.

Her world would never be the same again without him.

A little before dawn, Adam opened his eyes. Carrie, who had been watching for the slightest change, immediately bent over him. "How do you feel, Adam?"

His left hand went immediately to his right arm.

Touching his slightly cooler forehead, she smiled tremulously. "Yes, you still have both arms."

Her words woke the doctor. She stood as he approached the bed.

"My dear girl, perhaps you could give us a moment alone? And do send the good sergeant in to help me." All of Dr. Hastings' attention focused on his patient.

Chagrined at being pushed aside this way, she could only stare at Adam.

"I'm fine, Carrie. Please rest yourself." Although his words seemed to come with an effort, he managed a weak smile.

Carrie nodded and left to awaken Sergeant Young as he and Baker slept on opposite sides of the fireplace. After the young officer had joined the doctor and shut the door, she went inside her bedroom. Lying on the pallet she had prepared the evening before, she listened for any signs of being needed. Hearing none, exhaustion eventually overcame her, and she slept.

Pale morning light brightened the shadows in her room before she arose. After changing into a fresh dress, she brushed her hair, pinning the single braid in a circle on top of her head. She hoped to look her best for Adam. The only mirror remained in the cave, so there was no way to check her appearance.

Worried about Adam's condition, she stepped into the main room. The other bedroom door remained closed. No sign of the soldiers. They must have stored their knapsacks and weapons in the ambulance.

She peeked out the window at the impressive pile of chopped

wood in the front yard.

A dog barked nearby. With all the neighbors gone from the mountain or in hiding, it was an unusual sound in the past three months. She hoped it wasn't Star. He was supposed to be safely inside the cave with Jay.

The frantic barking grew closer. It was Star. The obedient dog didn't bark incessantly without good reason. Something must be wrong with Aunt Lavinia. Something Jay couldn't deal with.

The possibility spurred her into action. Her heart in her throat, she grabbed her cloak and ran into the yard. The ambulance was gone. She stared without comprehending. Had Baker moved the vehicle into the barn? Where was everyone? Didn't they hear Star, too?

Rushing back inside she burst into the closed bedroom door to check on Adam. His mattress lay empty.

With rising terror, she stared at the empty bed. Had he grown worse during the night? Where was he?

The room was empty. The house was empty. Dr. Hastings and his men were gone.

Where had they taken him?

Growing more fearful, Carrie ran outside to meet her dog.

She raced to the cave with Star at her side. As she drew closer she saw the limbs used to hide the entrance had been removed. Carrie stepped into the cave, her heart thudding even faster.

Baker stood with his back to her, hands raised. For a moment the darkness of the cave and the man's frozen posture confused her. Then, as her eyes adjusted, she saw Aunt Lavinia standing in the front room with a loaded rifle aimed at the Union soldier.

· CHAPTER TWELVE ·

tar immediately began to bark at the stranger inside the cave. Aunt Lavinia, clad in a faded purple dress, never took her eyes off the man as Carrie entered. Jay stood near his aunt, a frightened look on his face.

Carrie had never seen her little brother so scared. "Star, hush up."

The dog stopped barking, but remained watchful of the soldier.

"Aunt Lavinia, lower that rifle!" The wild look in her aunt's eyes scared her worse than the sight of the mountain crawling with soldiers. "This man is with the Union Army. He brought the surgeon to help Adam! He's a friend, Aunt Lavinia."

"He has no right to be here!" The hatred in her eyes chilled Carrie.

"I heard a rooster this morning while I was out hunting for downed trees to chop up for firewood for your family." His eyes darted from the rifle directed at him to the woman who held it. "I saw eggs in Carrie's basket last night, but didn't find any hens or farm animals in any of the buildings on the property. I figured chickens ran wild on the mountain. After I drove Adam and the doctor up to camp at dawn, I asked Sarge for a few minutes to find the chickens."

It felt as if all the air sucked out of Carrie's lungs. Adam was back at the camp.

"He didn't care as long as I shared. I wanted some eggs." Baker's flushed face betrayed his fear.

Aunt Lavinia's eyes narrowed. "I know what you wanted." One of the cows lowed from the back of the cave. "You wanted to steal our animals, take our food. Admit it!"

"Please, I meant no harm." Baker kept his gaze fastened on the loaded rifle as if contemplating his chances of taking control of the weapon. "I won't tell anybody you got cows and chickens."

Carrie took a step closer to her aunt. "See, he won't tell anybody about our animals."

"Pah! You'd believe a thieving Yankee?"

"Perhaps I can suggest a better plan."

Carrie swung around to face Sergeant Young as he entered the cave. "Sergeant! Yes, please, what is your suggestion?"

He took a couple of steps closer to Baker, his gaze fastened on the woman who held the weapon. "The army is in need of milk, eggs, and butter. We'd pay a good price for a continuous supply."

Carrie breathed a silent prayer at the possibility of a steady income. "See, Aunt Lavinia? They'll pay us."

As Aunt Lavinia stared at him, obviously wondering whether to trust his word, the young officer introduced himself and Baker.

"Please, Aunt Lavinia, we trusted Adam. He's a good man. We'll be treated fairly, won't we, Sergeant Young?"

Her aunt wavered, obviously aware of their desperate need for cash.

"You have my word on it." He spoke quietly, but with conviction. "I'll speak with the lieutenant. He'll see to it."

"It'd be just like me selling to our neighbors." Jay's green eyes pleaded with his aunt. "Please, Aunt Lavinia? Can't we sell to them?"

When she met her nephew's gaze, something relaxed in her expression. Loosening her hold on the rifle, she lowered it to the ground. "If Carrie agrees to a price, we'll do it."

Sergeant Young touched his cap respectfully. "Thank you, Ma'am."

Carrie walked across to the distraught woman. "How do you feel

Aunt Lavinia?"

"Can you help me back to bed, child? I'm all done in." All signs of anger vanished. All that remained was a woman in poor health, old before her time.

"Of course." Reaching out for her still shaking little brother, she hugged him closely with one arm while extending her other to her aunt. "I'll take care of you."

By the time Carrie had calmed her aunt and brother, it was midday. Drained of energy by her almost sleepless night and the dreadful scene at the cave, she could barely speak. Worried about Adam's recovery and the continued decline in her aunt, circumstances beyond her control threatened to weigh her down.

When she entered the main room of the cave, it surprised her to find the soldiers sitting near the entrance. Both men stood upon sighting her.

"Sergeant Young, I thought you both were back at the army camp by now." She flushed. "I apologize for what happened earlier. My aunt is ill. In fact, her health has noticeably declined in the past two months." She sighed. "I'd like to think she didn't plan to shoot you. She's not normally like this."

The sergeant listened respectfully. "Please, there's no need to speak of it again." He exchanged a glance with Baker, who nodded. "We did leave earlier. We went back to camp and retrieved the ambulance."

Hope of seeing Adam again caused her heart to beat faster. "Oh, did you bring Adam back? I'm happy to follow any instructions the doctor leaves for his care."

He shook his head regretfully. "Sorry, the doctor is concerned about Adam. He requires more care than you can give him in your home."

His words struck dread. "I didn't make him worse, did I?"

"I'm not a doctor, miss." The sergeant looked at her compassionately.

"But it looked to me like Adam received very loving care."

She flushed. Did the sergeant guess her love for his fellow comrade?

"No, we brought the ambulance to help you move back to your home."

The suggestion shocked her. With Union soldiers less than three miles away, that wasn't possible. Surely he realized it, too.

"Now that the army will be purchasing milk, eggs, and butter from you, there will be no reason to hide your livestock." He gestured the stony ceiling of the chilly, dimly lit cave. "Surely your aunt's health is affected by these surroundings. Your little brother will be happier, not to mention the livestock."

He made it sound so easy, but she knew it wasn't. "Even if the cabin is safe, I can't move Aunt Lavinia. She can only walk a few steps in her condition."

"Nothing could be simpler." He smiled. "We'll take the ambulance over until the path thins out too much. Items can be moved from the cave to the vehicle and your aunt can ride back, too."

It seemed like a lot of trouble. "Why do you want to do this for us?"

"You and your family might have saved Adam's life. It's still too soon to know if he'll recover from his wounds and live, but if he were healthy he'd do this for you. I know it."

He was right. Adam wouldn't want her hiding in this cave any longer than necessary.

It didn't take long to convince her aunt to return to their log cabin. The men worked quickly to transport the family's belongings from the cave to the farm. Meanwhile, Carrie and Jay escorted the livestock back to the barn and chicken coop.

Aunt Lavinia walked all the way to the ambulance and rode in relative comfort to her home.

Dusk was only an hour away when the men finished moving everything into the cabin. Sergeant Young and Baker wanted to be back at camp before fog descended. The officer arranged to purchase milk and eggs from them in two day's time.

Unable to focus on anything other than Adam, Carrie agreed. She tried to comfort herself with the thought that he'd be better cared for in the hospital, but it didn't alleviate her sorrow. She would visit him daily, no two ways about it. And when he felt better, maybe he could return to the cabin for a meal.

Moments before the men pulled away in the wagon to head back to their camp Carrie asked if it would be possible for her to see Adam the next day.

Baker gave her a concerned look. "I'm sorry, ma'am. I guess it wasn't clear earlier. The doctor wanted to get him to camp so he could be furloughed. His fever is worse. The doctor fears he might not survive if he remains in our field hospital. Adam is going home tomorrow by rail."

· Chapter Thirteen ·

he next couple of weeks crawled by. Baker stopped by every two days with a couple of other soldiers. They returned an empty milk urn and left with a full urn, eggs, and butter. They didn't pay with Confederate bills, but gave Carrie Union money that could be used at the commissary near the Union camp on Lookout Mountain or in Chattanooga.

Aunt Lavinia counted the cash after the soldiers left each time. The growing number of bills had a comforting effect on both women. They would be able to purchase items to replenish dwindling provisions—as long as supplies were available. Many items had been scarce for months, but they would make do. They always had.

Carrie always asked Baker for news of Adam but there was no word on whether he got home or died en route. Carrie tried not to think the worst but could not get the sight of his festering wound out of her mind or how tired Adam had looked before surgery. The rough road back to camp and then who knows how many days on a train … the image was too much to bear. Did he make it home? Even if he did, would she ever see him again? With winter setting in, chances were Adam would remain home throughout the winter. Baker explained that by then his unit would probably be fighting the Confederates elsewhere.

The memory of his kiss before his surgery haunted her. Even at the time, she feared he didn't believe he'd survive so the kiss held no promise for the future.

The possibility of never seeing him again robbed her of any happiness.

She had hoped that when he left, her heart would return to normal. It didn't happen. The heartache didn't diminish even with busy days.

With the work of the home and the increased amount of butter purchased by the soldiers, she had more than enough to occupy her time.

Even so, her thoughts and prayers never left Adam for more than a few minutes. Did he miss her? Did he ever think of her? She longed to see him, to find out for herself how he fared. She wondered if she would ever see him again. Could there be a future for a Union soldier and the daughter of a Confederate soldier?

One very good thing had come of the move back to the cabin. Aunt Lavinia's attitude improved. The courtesy of the Union soldiers had gone a long way toward easing her terrible bitterness. She often sat in a rocking chair in front of the fireplace for several hours, sewing squares of cloth to make quilts. Since the extra cloth stored in the cellar had been taken while they lived at the cave, Carrie had decided one of her first purchases would be fabric.

With Christmas just a couple of days away, Carrie anticipated purchasing a few items at the camp commissary. Although Baker had picked up the normal amount of dairy supplies this morning, he had requested to return the next day to buy all they could spare for Christmas meals. Carrie decided to accompany him and the other Union soldiers back to the camp. She could purchase supplies, but her main goal was to visit the hospital where Adam had stayed one night in the hopes of hearing news of him. There might even be enough money left to buy Jay a Christmas present.

There hadn't been any gifts last year.

But even with money for gifts, Christmas wouldn't be a time of joy. Not for her.

Not without Adam.

Shortly before noon on Christmas Eve Carrie grabbed an empty basket and climbed down from the wagon. The brisk wind blew open her cloak and chilled her. She thanked the soldiers for the ride up the steep mountain, complimenting them on the improvements they had made to the road in such a short amount of time. The jutting boulders were gone from the mountain road along with the deep ruts. The ride up the mountain had been smooth and pleasant, though a bit nippy.

They appreciated the compliments. It must have been hard work. Baker pointed toward one of the buildings used as the commissary as well as the hospital where Adam had lain the night before he left for home.

Carrie's gaze fastened on the former large home now serving as a hospital. She took a deep breath to calm her nerves. So many blue coats milling about. But none of them Adam.

She'd have to control her emotions. To him, she had been simply the girl who rescued and nursed him. Why, someone as special as him probably had a girl waiting for him back home. Yes, she remembered him talking about someone with Jay. Of course, he wanted to go home. What wounded soldier would not? Why had she ever entertained thoughts that he would marry her and stay on the mountain?

Stepping resolutely to the fine wooden door, she knocked.

A stranger opened the door and stared at her curiously.

"I ... I've been told this is the hospital where Mr. Hendricks stayed one night after his surgery."

He opened the door wider into what appeared to be the parlor of a wealthy homeowner. Men occupied several beds in the square room but it was the man standing beside the first bed, gathering his things, who captured her attention.

For a moment, Carrie feared for her sanity. She rubbed her eyes and looked again.

At the sound of her voice Adam turned his head so she only saw his profile. "Merry Christmas, Carrie." His broad smile lightened her agonized fear for him. "I didn't expect to see you on my first day back."

She gasped, hardly able to believe her eyes. "Oh, Adam, it's so good to see you. I ... we've been worried."

"I was in pretty bad shape after surgery. Doc Hastings sent me home on furlough because he thought I'd die in the field hospital." He frowned. "And most likely I would have. The infection got worse. Doctor back home said they almost lost me a couple of times. I don't remember much. Only that in order to save me they had to ... "

The light went out of his eyes. He pivoted further so that he now faced her.

Carrie's shocked gaze took in the empty sleeve of his blue uniform.

With his left hand he reached out and took hers. "They couldn't save my arm, Carrie. After you fought so hard for it, too." He gave her a tender glance. "I'll never forget how you stood up to everyone for my sake. My guardian angel."

She fought back tears. "Oh, Adam, I'm so ..." The words lodged in her throat with her unshed tears.

"Sorry?" His eyes searched hers. "Don't be. Sometimes God answers our prayers by making us less so he can be more. So we can be more for others, but in a different way."

It seemed an odd thing to say. "I don't understand. What do you mean?"

He dropped her hand and touched his empty sleeve. "I'll never be a soldier again. That's why I came back. I wanted to say goodbye to the men in my unit, my friends. But I'm done fighting."

The depth of his unhappiness was apparent in the way his smile sagged. "Adam, you lost an arm. You're not dead. You can do other things. Be a courier, a cook. Help in this hospital."

An awkward silence fell between them. He glanced around, as if waiting for her to say something more. Or leave.

What happened to the man who fought so hard to live? Was he really ready to just give up? All because of a lost limb?

A change of topic might help. "Jay will be thrilled to hear you're back on the mountain. Do you think you will have time to come visit?"

His smile briefly returned. "You know, I do miss that boy," he said with a chuckle. "When I was in the hospital back home I thought about what Jay told me about him wanting to be a doctor." His gaze shifted momentarily to the empty sleeve, then back to her face. "We could sure use more good ones. Baker said he'd drive me down to your house in the ambulance. I hope that will be okay."

"Of course. We'd love to have you over for a meal. Well, not Aunt Lavinia. You know how she feels about Yankees in her home. But I'll make sure she minds her manners."

He smiled and nodded. "I'd like that."

The awkwardness returned. She felt a wall between them that had never been there before today. Perhaps their friendship hadn't been as close as she had imagined. Maybe the real reason he came back wasn't just to say so long to the men in his unit, but to tell her good-bye for ever. He had yet to mention his girl back home. Was that on purpose? Was he hoping to avoid the topic?

And he had not kissed her. Had not even tried. What did she mean to him?

The misery in his eyes filled her heart with sadness.

"I'm not a whole man. If I can't fight for my country, what will I do?"

She couldn't believe her ears. "A great many things. How about farming or working for the railroad? How about getting married and raising a family?"

He glanced at her quickly and drew a deep breath at her last question. "Who would want me now?"

Anger seared through her. "Adam Hendricks, I'm ashamed of you! What if you can't lift some things or shoot a rifle or hold a baby with two arms? Do you think that matters? Do you really think any woman worth her salt would refuse to marry you for such a paltry reason?" She put her hands on her hips and glared at him.

Adam stepped closer, towering over her. There was a hopeful gleam in his eyes that had been missing moments before. "What about you, Carrie? Would you refuse to marry someone with a missing arm or leg?"

"That wouldn't be the reason *I* refused a proposal." She glared at him. "I'm surprised you would ask such a question."

"I hoped you'd say that." His left hand reached into his pants pocket and pulled out a small engagement ring. "Do you think you could ever love a Union soldier, Carrie Bishop?"

"I can't believe you'd ask me that."

"Well, can you?"

She covered his hand with hers as tears of joy filled her eyes. "Oh, I think that might be possible."

Cheers from every man in the room dazed Carrie as she stared radiantly up into Adam's eyes. The joy on his face was reflected in her heart.

"Carrie, when I kissed you last time, I believed myself to be at death's door. It really made me want to live." He grinned as she laughed happily. When their lips met, this time she felt the promise of the future.

He pulled back, kissed her a second time swiftly, and said softly, "When the doctor back home told me the infection had spread to the muscles and that I'd lose my arm I thought I was done for. Figured I'd be a half-man the rest of my life and no use to anyone. But then I remembered how you cared for me and I know with you by my side I'll be more of a man than I could ever be with both arms. Please, Carrie, say you'll be my wife."

As Adam slid his arm around her to hold her tightly, she buried her face in his chest. No place on earth had ever felt so much like home.

Placing her lips close to his ear, she whispered, "Yes, Adam Hendricks. I will be your Mrs. Hendricks. Only …" She pulled back and brushed away tears from her cheeks. "Don't tell Aunt Lavinia. At least, not right off." She looked up at him playfully. "If she finds out I'm marrying a Yankee it could start the battle of Lookout Mountain all over again."

Note from the Author

The battle fought on Lookout Mountain, under the command of Major General Joseph Hooker, became known as "The Battle Above the Clouds" for the dense fog that blanketed much of the mountain during the battle.

As part of my research for the Civil War, I read books written by Union and Confederate soldiers who lived through it. These gave me a wonderful sense of everyday camp life, battles, and the men's reactions to the war. Two of these books provided wonderful details for this story.

The first is *My Life in the Irish Brigade: The Civil War Memoirs of Private William McCarter, 116th Pennsylvania Infantry*, edited by Kevin E. O'Brien. William McCarter is shot in the arm during the Battle of Fredericksburg. A piece of the bullet was removed hours after the battle. This provided instant relief, but part of the bullet and seventeen bone fragments remained. The wound didn't close and months later his doctor told William that he preferred it stay open until all the broken bones worked out of it, which took almost four years. His arm healed but was never as strong again.

As far as our story is concerned, I really wanted Adam to keep his arm. The doctor agreed to go the extra mile to try and save it because he didn't have other patients clamoring for his attention. He didn't feel the prospects were good for Adam keeping the arm, and he was right. Infection quickly set in and he lost it. Unfortunately, this was a reality for far too many Civil War soldiers.

The second Civil War soldier who influenced me wrote *Memoirs of a Dutch Mudsill: The "War Memories" of John Henry Otto, Captain, Company D, 21st Regiment Wisconsin Volunteer Infantry*, edited by David Gould and James B. Kennedy. John Otto was in Chattanooga during the siege. He described the starvation of the men and the joy of the soldiers who lined the Tennessee River as boats brought food for the troops. The men were so starved that they overate. It created stomach complaints. A few even died. Along with the 78th Pennsylvania, John's 21st Wisconsin regiment was assigned to camp on Lookout Mountain on December 2, 1863. They stayed near a resort village that he called "Summerville," though other sources referred to it as "Summertown." He also talked about Union sympathizers who lived in caves on the mountain. These families had moved everything they could into the caves with them. Whatever they left in their homes was gone when they returned. Now that Union soldiers occupied the mountain, they felt free to roam about again. John arranged to buy wine from one of these men.

All of the speaking characters in this book are fictional except one. I used John Otto as the lieutenant in the Union camp that Carrie visits. I wanted to thank him for providing so much wonderful information in this small way.

All of the generals, divisions, and regiments in the story were in Chattanooga. A few accounts talked about Brigadier General Whitaker drinking before the battle. As this would have been Adam's first time to serve under him, he would surely have noticed this in his commanding officer.

Most people left when armies occupied their town during the Civil War, even if they supported that army's side. Big and small battles erupted where soldiers went, and innocent bystanders could easily be hurt or killed. Though the leaders preferred townspeople to leave, some stayed. There were folks too ill to travel. Others had nowhere to go or were too poor to leave.

To research this story, my husband and I traveled to Chattanooga. We visited Point Park Battlefield and The Battles for Chattanooga Electric Map & Museum on Lookout Mountain. The view is breathtaking from the Point Park Battlefield, part of the Chickamauga and Chattanooga National Military Park. Standing next to the cannons near the cliffs, I tried to imagine the feelings of those who defended and those who attacked. If you are interested in learning more, this may be a good place for a weekend visit.

Thanks for going back with me to 1863 and spending time on Lookout Mountain. I hope that we meet again on another battlefield or a different historical setting.

Sandra Merville Hart

Acknowledgements

The author wishes to thank Paul McDonell at The Battles of Chattanooga Electric Map & Museum in Lookout Mountain, Tennessee, for his willingness to answer questions about the battle and Chattanooga area history.

Many thanks go to Julie Gwinn, editor, for her encouragement and helpful suggestions to strengthen the story. The author also appreciates the support of Barbara King and Michele Creech, author representatives. Thanks to Eddie Jones, Lighthouse Publishing of the Carolinas, for the opportunity to publish this story. The author wishes to thank her agent, Joyce Hart of Hartline Literary Agency, who believed in her first.

The author extends grateful appreciation to writer and author friends who added to the success of the book in various ways. The list includes: Lisa Carter, Daphne Woodall, Marianne Jordan, Terri Kelly, Erin Unger, Becky McGurrin, Felicia Bowen Bridges, Phyllis Freeman, Mary Ellis, Rosanna Huffman, Carole Brown, Sharon Lavy, Michelle Levigne, Catherine Castle, Angie Arndt, Tamera Lynn Kraft, Rebecca Waters, Ane Mulligan, Lena Nelson Dooley, and Katherine M. Pasour, PhD.

Special thanks go to my family and friends for their love and support. I love you all.

Made in the USA
Monee, IL
27 January 2023

26155863R00059